"It's not funny, Kit. If anything happened to you…"

He raised himself up on one elbow and looked searchingly at her. He reached for her arm, gripping it gently. "If anything happened to me, then what?"

She could hardly think with him touching her. "I don't want to think about it."

"What don't you want to think about?" he pressed. "What are you afraid of?"

"I—I wouldn't want you to get hurt protecting me." Her stammer was a dead giveaway that her emotions were in turmoil.

"I wouldn't want anything to happen to either of us. For you to get hurt on my watch is unthinkable to me. Come here. Let's talk about it." He pulled her forward until she fell against him on the floor. He gathered her closer and entangled their legs.

"Kit—" She half gasped his name.

"On second thought, I don't feel much like talking." He lowered his mouth to hers. Natalie had been wanting this for so long she was past considering the wisdom of it. Kit started kissing her with a hunger as great as her own. In an explosion of need she began kissing him back, forgetting everything as she poured out her feelings for him.

Dear Reader,

Sometimes on the news you hear about something that sounds so unbelievable, you shudder and are grateful it never happened to you. My heroine in *The Texas Ranger's Family* is such a person, a mother with a child going along living her life the best she can.

But her world explodes when little by little everything she thought to be true turns out to be a lie. She's forced to question if anything in her life was ever real. Her disillusion starts when her husband dies and an attractive Texas Ranger shows up at her back door to inform her she's been married to a killer who's been on the FBI's most wanted list for years.

Nothing fascinates me more than the expert way the Texas Rangers go about solving a case. This third book in the Lone Star Lawmen series shows once again why their fame is legendary, and also why these two people are so heroic, they belong together to form a new and lasting family.

Enjoy!

Rebecca Winters

THE TEXAS RANGER'S FAMILY

———

REBECCA WINTERS

⊞ HARLEQUIN® AMERICAN ROMANCE®

Recycling programs
for this product may
not exist in your area.

ISBN-13: 978-0-373-75617-9

The Texas Ranger's Family

Printed in U.S.A.

Chapter One

Texas Ranger Kit Saunders took cover behind a fat pine tree and watched with his binoculars from a distance. Seven people accompanied the honey-blonde widow standing at the grave site at the Evergreen Cemetery on this hot July afternoon in Austin.

The woman was Natalie Harris, and her husband, Rodney Parker Harris, age thirty-three, was being laid to rest. As far as any of the mourners, including his widow, knew, the deceased had been an accountant with LifeSpan Pharmaceutical, a huge private corporation in Austin. A week ago he'd been found at the low-end Sleepy Hollow Hotel, dead of a gunshot wound to the temple.

Kit's captain, T. J. Horton, had assigned him to the case only yesterday.

The police had run the victim's DNA through the database and, according to their report, the name Rodney Harris was the latest in a string of aliases. The name on the deceased's original birth certificate was that of escaped felon Harold Park from Colorado, who'd disappeared eight years ago.

Park was on the FBI's Most Wanted list. After serving only two years of a sixty-year sentence for murder, embezzlement, armed robbery and grand larceny, he and another prisoner, convicted killer Alonzo Morales, had escaped during a transfer from the ADX Federal Penitentiary in Florence, Colorado, to Canaan Federal Prison in Pennsylvania. Since that time both fugitives had gone by many false names that prevented the Feds from recapturing them.

The preliminary report from the detective here in Travis County suggested the gunshot wound was self-inflicted, but nothing would be official until all the forensic evidence had been reviewed. Something didn't add up in Kit's mind. It didn't make sense that the felon would kill himself. A clever killer could have set it up to look like suicide.

A search of Harold-alias-Rod's bank records revealed that $400,000 had been deposited into his checking account one day and withdrawn the next. The day after that, he'd been found dead in his hotel room. The size and date of the large deposit were inconsistent with his earnings from the pharmaceutical company, and the abrupt withdrawal was just plain suspicious. Normally that kind of money would have been put in a money market or the stock market at least.

Since Harold-alias-Rod had crossed state lines and had been an armed, dangerous killer, the police had asked for the Texas Rangers to take over. These were early days in the case. The police report also stated that Mrs. Harris had hired an attorney who'd attempted to serve him with divorce papers on the day he was shot.

Since they weren't yet divorced and he'd absconded with money she had half rights to under property laws, it appeared she could have a motive to see him dead.

But if Harris had still been living a life of crime and the money was stolen, then there may have been accomplices involved—maybe even other ex-felons from his past life—who might be potential culprits. If the widow was innocent of any wrongdoing, then she herself might be a target for interested parties still looking for the missing money.

Kit hadn't met Natalie Harris. The only information he had on her so far was that she was a twenty-eight-year-old pharmacist and had a sixteen-month-old daughter named Amy. There was no sign of the toddler at the graveside.

He was going to have to build this case from scratch. Knowing of the service today, he'd decided to study the people who showed up and take pictures with a long-range lens. Oftentimes a murderer appeared at the funeral to gloat. Of the seven people present, two were females, but he didn't sense they were family. He had the rap sheet on Alonzo Morales with a mug shot and would know if he saw that face again.

Before long the people assembled at the burial turned to leave and go their separate ways. Kit's first frontal view of Mrs. Harris being helped by the mortuary staff came as a shock to his senses. She was a true beauty; maybe five foot six. He took a picture of her. The classy, tailored black suit couldn't disguise the mold of her shapely body and legs. Everything about her appealed to him, which came as a shock. It had been a long time since he had reacted this way to a total stranger.

Kit didn't know what he'd expected. Maybe to find a widow in tears? But from a distance he got the impression she hadn't given in to whatever emotion she was feeling. Her lovely classic bone structure was undermined by features that showed no animation. Shock could do that to a person in mourning.

But since she'd filed for divorce, maybe she'd passed through her period of grief long before the papers had been served. Whether elated he was dead at her hands, relieved he was gone by another person's doing, or sad or even haunted by the way he'd died, the frozen mask he saw in front of him revealed no secrets.

Was he staring at a killer? If he was close enough to look into her eyes, he might be able to get a feel for what was going on in her psyche.

His gaze followed her to a silver Toyota parked on the roadside. The clergyman helped her in before walking to the car ahead of hers. Little by little everyone drove away from the cemetery, leaving the workers to finish their jobs.

Kit would give her a half hour before he phoned to set up a time to meet, preferably before the day was out. He needed to know her background. Was she a home-grown Texan? How long had she known the man she'd married? What about her parents or siblings? The police report didn't have many details about her background and a dozen questions filled his mind.

Tonight he planned to drive to Marble Falls to watch his younger brother, Brandon, compete in the steer wrestling event at the Charley Taylor Rodeo Arena. Brandon was headed for a world championship competition in Las Vegas this coming December and Kit was excited for him. Until he'd made the decision to go into law enforcement, Kit had competed big-time in the same sport. But when he'd made up his mind to follow in his father's footsteps, he'd given up the rodeo and ended up losing his girlfriend Janie at the same time. She knew that the Saunders brothers had suffered over the loss of their Texas Ranger father in a shootout when they were fifteen and seventeen. Fearing the same thing would happen to Kit, she'd broken it off with him, not wanting any part of a career that could end his life right in the middle of it, leaving a grieving wife and children.

Five years ago Janie had fallen in love with Brandon's hazer, Scott Turner, and they'd married. As of today they had one child. He was happy for her. Any residual pain from their breakup had disappeared a long time ago. When all was said and done, he was content enough with his bachelor existence. His mother and brother needed support and he could be there for them.

Kit would be thirty-one next month. He liked being single and free of emotional baggage. Out of his three best friends in the Rangers, two of them, Cy and Vic, were now married and incredibly happy. That left him and Luckey, who'd been married for a short time before his wife had decided she hated what he did for a living. Their divorce had pretty well scarred him.

Kit was thankful he'd avoided that problem before vows had been said. Janie had done both of them a huge favor. From time to time since then he'd gone out with various women, but no one female after Janie had made a lasting impression.

He made his way back to his truck and started up the engine, driving out of the cemetery to the main road and heading for his town house at Chimney Corners in Northwest Austin. Oddly enough Mrs. Harris lived in the same part of the city; no great distance from his condo. That would cut down his driving time. He'd grab a bite to eat and then make the call. If he could interview her soon, he'd leave for Marble Falls and pick up his mom en route to the arena. It would be good to spend some time with family.

NATALIE PULLED HER Toyota Corolla into the driveway and pressed the remote. She was still getting used to entering the garage devoid of Rod's white Sentra. The police had impounded it when they'd investigated the crime scene at the hotel a week ago.

But the second the garage door lifted, she realized someone had been there since she'd left for the graveside service. The lawn mower and equipment for the yard had been moved around. Items from the shelf, including a Christmas tree stand, had been thrown on the cement floor, preventing her from driving in. What on earth?

Frightened that a burglar had broken into her house, she backed out to the street and parked along the curb a few houses away to call Detective Carr. He'd been the one who'd come to see her following Rod's shooting in the hotel where he'd been living temporarily. The detective had told her to call him if she needed anything.

Her hand shook as she waited for him to answer. "Mrs. Harris?"

"Yes. I'm so glad you're there. I just got home from the service to find my garage in disarray. I think someone has broken into my house. He could still be inside."

"Where are you?"

"In my car, parked down the street."

"What make and color?"

"A silver Corolla."

"Stay right there. Officers will be at your home within minutes."

"Thank y-you," she stammered and hung up. There'd been too many shocks already and now this...

She sat there trembling as she stared at her house, watching to see if someone would come out. Before long, two police cars arrived. Three officers got out and started casing the place, and the fourth walked toward her car. She rolled down the window.

"Mrs. Harris?"

"Yes. Thank you for coming."

"If I could have a key to your home, we'll check inside."

She pulled her keys out of the ignition and gave him the one that would unlock the front door. "There's a crawlspace under the house. You have to get to it through the laundry room. Someone could be hiding in there."

"We'll check. Stay right where you are."

Natalie nodded and waited. There were several cars

parked on each side of the street. Any one of them could be the intruder's. After several minutes the same officer came back outside.

"Whoever ransacked your house is gone." He handed back her key. "Please pull into your driveway, but stay in the car until you hear from Detective Carr. He'll follow up and give you instructions."

"Okay. Thanks for coming so quickly."

No sooner did she watch the police drive away than her phone rang. She clicked it on. "Detective Carr?"

"Mrs. Harris?"

The deep, attractive male voice didn't sound like anyone she knew. "Yes?"

"This is Miles Saunders with the Texas Rangers." Natalie's heart skipped a beat. Why was a Texas Ranger phoning her? She thought they only worked on big federal cases. "Detective Carr contacted me. I hear you've been burglarized while you were attending your husband's graveside service."

"Yes."

"I'm about six minutes away. Leave your car in the driveway and go into the house through your garage. I'll park on the next street over and walk through a few neighbors' yards to knock on your back door. Use a hand towel to open it. Don't touch anything. A forensics team will arrive right away to go through everything. They'll come to your front door."

"A-all right."

She heard the click as he disconnected, still unable to believe what was happening. She knew there were unscrupulous people who read through the obituaries and chose to break into people's homes on the day of a funeral.

Taking a deep breath, she started her car and pulled into her driveway. She got out and entered the house through the garage as instructed, passing through the small laundry room into the kitchen. Cupboards were open and foodstuffs were on the floor.

Natalie had only been gone two hours, but it looked as though a wrecking ball had been at work. As she walked through her two-bedroom rambler, she saw that drawers and closets had been ransacked. Her bedding had been thrown on the floor and her mattress lay halfway off the box spring. Numerous items lay strewed on the floor of both bathrooms. She checked the nursery and found it in shambles. Some intruder had gone through every room, causing total upheaval.

She was wild with anger. Last evening after returning from her work at the pharmacy, she'd thoroughly cleaned the rambler in case someone dropped by after the graveside service. The house would be neat, clean and filled with flowers.

She'd inherited this house from her deceased mother, and she and Rod had made it into their home. But their marriage had started to fall apart soon after Amy was born, and now he was dead and her family home was a disaster.

Half a dozen floral arrangements had arrived during the week, but several of them had been knocked over. Water had spilled on the carpet. The fireplace screen had been knocked over. Cushions were piled on the floor in the living room and den. The drawers of her computer desk had been pulled out, the contents dumped on the floor. Several framed prints had been taken off the walls and the backings torn. Whoever had gone through her house had been desperately looking for something.

While she waited for the Ranger, she reached again for her cell and placed a call to Jillian.

Her good friend lived just across the street and had been looking after Amy since Natalie had gone back to work. The little girl was good company for Jillian's eighteen-month-old daughter, Susie, and the arrangement allowed Jillian to earn a little extra money while her husband, Bart, served another tour of duty overseas with the marines.

"Jillian? You're not going to believe this," Natalie said when her friend answered. "I just got home from the service and found that my house has been broken into"

"You're kidding!"

"I wish I were. Life has been a nightmare since I got that call from the police about Rod. Can you keep Amy a little longer? I have to wait for some Ranger to come over."

"What? Why?"

"I have no idea. And a forensics team. As soon as they're gone, I'll be over to get her."

"Don't you worry about anything. There's no hurry."

"Yes, there is. You've gone beyond the call of duty to watch her on a Saturday afternoon. That wasn't our arrangement. I plan to pay you double."

"Natalie—don't be ridiculous. You've been through a horrible experience. What are friends for?"

"You're the best, Jillian. I'll be over as soon as I can."

The second she hung up, Natalie's landline rang, startling her. She moved to the kitchen to answer it but checked the caller ID first. It was blank. Would it be one of those hang-up calls she'd gotten twice this week already?

Natalie hated to answer without knowing who was on the other end, especially after this break-in, although it could be one of many important calls she was expecting—the police, the bank, the attorney, the mortuary, her boss at work, her coworkers, church friends, her insurance agent. But right now she was in no state to talk to anyone and let it ring until the person on the other end gave up or left a message.

She looked around but couldn't tell if anything was missing. She'd developed a bad headache and needed a pain pill.

One look in the bathroom mirror made her realize she needed to freshen up before the Ranger arrived and she washed her face, remembering too late that she wasn't supposed to touch anything. The burial plot in the newer section of the cemetery hadn't been planted with shade trees yet. The heat had caused her to break out in perspiration, but she didn't have time to change out of her lightweight linen suit.

After drying her face, Natalie refreshed her lipstick and gave her tousled, collarbone-length hair a good brushing. When she heard the knock on the back door, her brush fell to the floor. Her nerves were that bad.

She walked down the hall, past the nursery and into the kitchen. She used a dish towel to open the door leading to the backyard. Whatever picture of the Ranger she'd had in her mind didn't come close to the sight of the tall, thirtyish, hard-muscled male in a Western shirt, jeans and cowboy boots.

Her gaze flitted over his dark brown hair only to collide with his beautiful hazel eyes appraising her through a dark fringe of lashes.

"Mrs. Harris? Miles Saunders." She felt the stranger's probing look pierce her before he displayed his credentials. That's when she noticed the star on his shirt pocket.

This man is the real thing. The stuff that made the Texas Rangers legendary. She had the strange feeling that she'd seen him somewhere before, but shrugged it off. This was definitely the first time she'd ever met a Ranger.

"Come in." Her voice faltered, mystified by this unexpected visit. She was pretty sure the Rangers didn't investigate a home break-in.

"Thank you." He took a few steps on those long, powerful legs. His presence dominated the kitchen. She invited him to follow her into the living room.

"Please sit down." She indicated the upholstered chair on the other side of the coffee table while she took the matching chair. There was no place else to sit until the room was put back together.

He did as she asked. "I understand you have a daughter. Is she here?"

The man already knew quite a bit about her, she realized. "No. I left her with my sitter who lives across the street."

He studied one of the framed photos that hadn't been knocked off the end table, even though a drawer had been pulled out. "She looks a lot like you, especially the eyes. She's a little beauty."

Natalie looked quickly at the floor, stunned by the personal comment. He'd sounded sincere. So far everything about him surprised her so much she couldn't think clearly.

He turned to focus his attention on Natalie. "You're very composed for someone who's been through so much. Your husband's funeral was just this afternoon, wasn't it?"

"I'm trying to hold it together. If you'd taken any longer to get here, you might have found a screaming lunatic on your hands." She was nervous and talking too fast, but she couldn't help it. "Why would the Texas Rangers want to talk to me? I already answered the detective's questions after they found my husband's body at the hotel. It's hard for me to believe he took his own life, but even more difficult to believe anyone would have wanted to kill him."

"Why do you think it wasn't a suicide?"

Averting her eyes she said, "In my opinion he was too selfish to do it. That's what I told the police. Now I've probably shocked you."

"Not at all. Tell me something. Was your husband right- or left-handed?"

"Left."

"The report said the gun was found in his left hand, but the angle of the bullet raises some questions. Your answer convinces me the gunshot wasn't self-inflicted."

She sat back in the chair. "So someone killed him? Am I a suspect?"

"If this weren't crucial, I wouldn't have insisted on talking to you today. I'll explain, but we're going to need some time, unless you want me to come back this evening."

"No, no." Might as well get this over with. "I'll call my sitter and prepare her for a longer wait. Excuse me." Natalie got up from the chair and hurried into the kitchen to call her friend on her cell phone.

"Don't hate me for this, Jillian, but the Ranger is here now and it sounds like this is going to take a while longer."

"You poor thing."

"It's all a little scary. Would you mind keeping Amy? I hate to do this to you, but he's made it sound like it's really important."

"The girls are playing in the toy room and having a great time. Don't worry about us. I'll give them both dinner. You take your time."

"Bless you, Jillian."

She hung up and rushed back to the living room.

The Ranger eyed her directly. "I know you're full of questions, so I'll get to the point. Your husband's death was a homicide. But that's not the whole of it."

She knit her hands together. "What do you mean?"

"The police stumbled onto some information that has resulted in the case being handled by the Texas Rangers. My captain has assigned it to me. That's why the detective informed me of your phone call instead of following through himself."

"I still don't understand." Something told her she wasn't going to like what he told her.

His expression sobered. "Your husband wasn't the man he claimed to be."

Her adrenaline surged. "What do you mean exactly?"

"I wish there was a way to soften the blow for you. The man you knew as Rodney Parker Harris was actually born Harold Bartlett Park. He was born and raised in Denver, Colorado."

She felt as if her lungs froze while the revelation sank in. "Surely you're mistaken!"

"DNA doesn't lie. His grandparents raised him after his parents were killed in a car crash when he was seven, but they couldn't control him. In his teens he ran away and got into serious trouble. In time he used various aliases and committed crimes that put him in prison for a sixty-year sentence."

"Sixty?" Her cry resounded in the room.

"That's right. He'd only served two of them when he escaped eight years ago during a prisoner transfer to another facility. He eventually ended up here in Austin. There's been an arrest warrant out on him for years."

A gasp escaped her lips. She sprang to her feet. "You're telling me that I was married to a *felon*?"

His eyes looked at her with compassion. "I'm afraid so. You're welcome to see the DNA test results. They prove he's the same man who'd been on his way to another prison when he made his escape with a fellow inmate. That killer is still at large."

Fear raced through her as her thoughts leaped ahead. "Do you think he's the one who broke in here?"

"In time I'll find out who did this."

She shivered as he pulled a paper from his back pocket and handed it to her. "This is what we call a rap sheet."

Her fingers trembled as she opened it. Another cry resounded in the room as she saw the mug shot of the man she'd been married to. It was Rod, but a younger Rod with long black hair and a beard. The good-looking man she'd fallen in love with had short-cropped, dark blond hair and was clean-shaved.

Natalie looked down the list of his crimes that had earned him a sixty-year prison sentence. *"Murder?"* The knowledge that she'd been living with a hard-core criminal caused her to break out in a cold sweat. This was her precious Amy's father?

Her hands went clammy.

Horrified, she dropped the paper and ran to the bathroom where she threw up. When there was nothing left, she rinsed out her mouth and brushed her teeth. To her shock she saw the Ranger waiting for her in the hall while she clung to the sink to recover.

"I wish there'd been an easier way to break this to you," he murmured. "If you want to lie down, I understand."

His kindness got to her. She let go of the sink. "I'd like to pretend none of this is real, but I know it is or you wouldn't be here. No wonder the Texas Rangers are involved. Since I was in the process of divorcing him, I'm sure the police have already decided I killed him."

She left the bathroom and walked to the living room on shaky legs.

"They have to look at a death from every angle." His brows lifted. "Do you own a firearm?"

"No."

"Did your husband?"

She took a steadying breath. "Not that I ever knew about."

He eyed her speculatively through veiled eyes. "Why do *you* think the police would automatically assume you wanted him dead?"

"Because he'd been unfaithful to me. Now that I know the truth about him, it wouldn't surprise me if he'd been with different women throughout our marriage. This is unbelievable." She couldn't disguise the tremor in her voice. "When I had proof of his infidelity, I told him I was filing for divorce and asked him to leave the house."

"How did he handle that?"

"He didn't take me seriously until I warned him I'd call the police to put a restraining order on him. To my surprise he actually packed up and left. It almost seemed too easy, but it makes sense if he knew the FBI was hunting for him."

The Ranger shifted his weight. "Mrs. Harris, the detective's opinion of what happened was only speculation while he investigated your husband's case. It was turned over to me too quickly for any conclusions to be drawn. I haven't seen all the forensic evidence yet. Now that I'm in charge, I prefer to investigate the facts without bringing any bias from other sources. That's why it was so important I spoke with you today. For the time being we're going to keep any more information from being leaked to the press."

"Thank you for that."

"You've received a shock—you're still pale. Sit down and I'll fix you a cup of coffee."

She pressed her lips together. "I imagine you could use some, too. Come into the kitchen. I'll answer your questions while I make it. I need to stay busy." Her suggestion coincided with the doorbell ringing.

"That'll be the team. I'll let them in."

"They'll need to check the garage, too."

"I'll tell them. I also want them to take your fingerprints. I hope that's all right."

He left her long enough to go to the door. Three people, two men and a woman, came in carrying equipment. They put on latex gloves and got to work. After meeting Natalie, one of the men took impressions of her fingers at the kitchen table while the other two checked the room for other prints.

When that was done they went about their business through the rest of the house, dusting surfaces and looking for evidence. The moment was surreal.

The Ranger stepped over several items on the floor to sit at the table. The high chair stood in the cor-

ner. She felt his gaze while she fixed coffee for them.
"Where do you want to start?"

"Before we begin, you need to know I'll be recording our conversation."

Natalie nodded. "Do you take cream or sugar?"

"Both."

So did she. She prepared two mugs and brought
them to the table, sitting opposite him. After being
sick to her stomach, the coffee tasted good, the sugar
reviving her. He appeared to enjoy his, too, draining
most of his mug before sitting back.

"Tell me about yourself first. I saw two women at
the graveside service."

"You were there?" she asked in disbelief.

"Watching from a distance. Were either of them
your relatives?"

"No. I am an only child and my mother died several
years ago. My parents divorced when I was twelve.
My father had an affair and married the woman. They
moved to his hometown in Canada. I never saw or
heard from him again."

"You've been through a lot of heartache in your
life," he observed with empathy. "Now, I'd like you
to tell me about how you met your husband, and I'll
also need you to identify the people in these photos
for me." He handed her the camera and she blinked
when she saw the display, astonished that he'd taken
pictures at the cemetery. She swiped her finger across
the screen, scrolling through the images before giving
him back the camera.

She stared into space. "My husband and I met just

over two and a half years ago. It was November. A controlled-substance delivery from LifeSpan Pharmaceutical didn't check with the head pharmacist's order. The shipment usually comes in a brown box with tamper-proof tape. When I saw that the wrong order had been delivered, I called the plant. Several conversations took place before a man in accounting came on the line. It was Rod.

"He said the problem would be taken care of. The next thing I knew he came to the pharmacy with the correct shipment."

"Where do you work?"

"In the pharmacy at the Grand Central store on Spruce Street, about a mile from here."

"How long have you been a pharmacist?"

"I received my degree seven years ago and I've been working there ever since. The head pharmacist, John Willard, and his wife, Marva, were two of the people at the service today."

"Tell me about the other woman who was there. The older one."

"Ellen Butterworth is a woman from the church who was good friends with my mother."

"I see. All right, back to your story about Rod."

"I thought it was unusual that someone from the accounting department would make the delivery instead of a courier, but Rod reminded me that we'd spoken on the phone once before about a separate issue. He told me he liked the sound of my voice and wondered what I was like, so he'd taken it upon himself to bring the package in person."

"You'd never met him in person before?"

"No. But now that I know he was a criminal, it wouldn't surprise me if he'd seen me somewhere and found out about me ahead of time."

"It wouldn't surprise me, either. Go on."

"Rod came by several times after that and talked me into going out to lunch with him. I was flattered. He was very kind when I told him about my mother's battle with MS. She'd only just died before he came into my life. I found him attractive and we started dating. I learned that he'd been in the military but had been released from service when he was wounded in the lower leg."

"Did you see any proof of his military service?"

"No. I had no reason to question it. He said that during his time in the military, his folks were killed in a car crash in Houston, where he'd been born and raised. The military had helped him find a job from their outreach program and he was interviewed by LifeSpan to work in their accounting department. In time he'd moved his way up and eventually became the director of Finance. One thing led to another and he asked me to marry him."

Her gaze flicked to his. "After looking at that rap sheet, I can see that everything he told me was a spectacular work of fiction." She shook her head. "His healed gunshot wound had to have come from another source that had nothing to do with fighting a war."

"Not the war he described to you. He was injured fleeing arrest after he escaped."

She groaned. "Here I've been living with a killer,

thinking all along how horrible combat must have been for him. He fed me lie after lie and I believed him."

"Harold Park was a consummate sociopath who fooled everyone, including his employers."

The Texas Ranger was trying to make her feel better, but the fact that Harold had lied to more people than just her gave Natalie no comfort.

Chapter Two

"What is it they say? Truth is stranger than fiction?" Natalie's voice quivered. *"The lies..."* She couldn't believe it.

The Ranger nodded and she saw the concern in his eyes. "A good con artist can charm his way into just about anything he wants. He must have wanted you badly. The man worked his way into LifeSpan using fraudulent documents created by a master forger. Harold was the best at what he did."

A shudder swept through her body. "And my mother had just passed away. I was at my most vulnerable." Bitterness welled up inside her. "I fell into his lap like the proverbial apple dropping from the tree. He knew a good thing when he saw it...a woman all alone with her own house paid for and a good job. Exactly the right kind of person for a fugitive to marry to hide his past life of crime."

"Don't go there, Mrs. Harris. He was too clever to give himself away to anyone—he'd eluded the police for years. His mistake was getting caught with another woman. When did you realize it?"

She moistened her lips. "Amy had just turned a year old and I'd planned a little evening party for her with the idea that Rod could be there when he got home from work. But he didn't make it. He called me and said he'd been detained in a meeting but he'd make it up to us. I'd been putting up with those kinds of excuses from the time she was born, but that was the moment it occurred to me my husband was slipping away from me.

"About a month later I called him at work and found out he wasn't there and hadn't been in all day. I knew something was going on he didn't want me to know about."

A grimace marred the Ranger's rugged features. "Did you finally confront him?"

"Yes. About two and a half months ago I was having lunch with my best friend from college. She and her husband live in Arizona, but they'd flown in to attend a friend's wedding and we got together. She happened to mention that she'd bumped into Rod at the short-term airport parking. He'd told her he was dropping off my cousin for a flight."

Natalie shot Saunders a glance. "I don't have a cousin. He'd told my friend a blatant lie. At that point I knew in my heart he'd been having an affair, maybe even several."

After a silence he said, "What's your friend's name and phone number? I'd like to speak to her."

"Colette Barnes. She's in Phoenix." Natalie opened the contacts folder in her cell phone and found him the number.

"Did your husband admit to the affair when you confronted him?"

She bit her lip. "Yes. He was amazingly forthright about it. He accused me of having lost interest in him after Amy was born. It was a lie. He accused me of going back to work to avoid him. That *wasn't* a lie. I needed to get back to the job I knew because intuition told me our marriage wasn't going to make it." She took a deep breath. "It was my mother's story all over again. An unfaithful husband who didn't want to deal with his child."

"Except that your story wasn't your mother's, not by a long shot. A dangerous killer used you. The circumstances aren't comparable. When did you go back to work?"

"Two months ago."

"When you first mentioned divorce, what did he say?"

"He looked all penitent and said he didn't want one. Rod claimed the woman meant nothing to him. He promised never to see her again, but by then I was done. He was so cold and hadn't shown real remorse for any of his behavior, including missing his daughter's first birthday. I couldn't understand it and felt like I'd never known him. Now I know why," she reflected with a heavy heart.

"I've seen his type before. He's the kind that never formed emotional attachments early in life."

She nodded. "He's exactly like that. Later on that night I asked him to pack up and leave the house. I told him I was going to hire an attorney and he'd need one, too. Though the house is in my name, he threatened that he was eligible for half the property and would sue me for it.

"That's when I knew I'd married a stranger. If he wanted to fight over the house he'd never paid for without any concern for his daughter's future, there was no hope for us. I told him we'd have to work out everything in court. But he died before that day came." She paused for a moment. "I never wished him dead, but he's been dead to me for a long time."

Before the Ranger could say anything, the head of the forensics team came into the kitchen to say they were through. Saunders walked them to the front door, where they talked for a few minutes. After they filed out, he turned his attention back to Natalie.

"It turns out that whoever invaded your home must have had a key. There's no sign of a break-in."

"Maybe it was that other inmate you were talking about."

"Maybe, maybe not. But either way I'd say that's enough questions for now. I'll help you clean up your house before I leave."

"Oh, no. That won't be necessary, but thank you."

He zeroed in on her with his gaze. "I insist. Until the surveillance team arrives, I'm not letting you out of my sight."

A chill ran down her spine. "Surveillance?"

"Absolutely. I'm having you and your house guarded around the clock."

Her heart thudded with anxiety. "So you think I'm in danger, then?"

"Rod was a career felon. He could have enemies who wouldn't hesitate to hurt you or your daughter."

"But why?"

"Come on, let's get your place cleaned up while we talk. If you'll give me a towel, I'll get the water out of the carpet."

"You don't need to do that."

"I want to."

She couldn't budge him. In the end she found him a towel that had been thrown on the floor next to the linen closet. "Here you go. I'll clean up the nursery then I'll go for Amy. Jillian needs to be relieved—she's been such a help. I think I'll take her one of these floral arrangements, maybe that large one with the daisies and roses."

"They're beautiful. Who sent them?"

"My boss. The one from the photo. John Willard. He and his wife have proved to be terrific friends."

The Ranger got down on one knee to perform his task and Natalie's eyes lingered on the striking picture of virility he made. She decided he must be a man in a million to pitch in when he didn't have to. She tore herself away and hurried to Amy's room to put everything back in place. When she returned to the living room, she found it and the den restored and in perfect order, with nearly all traces of water gone.

She discovered her guest in the kitchen, washing his hands. When he looked over his shoulder at her, she smiled. "If I didn't know better, I'd think you'd been sent from Hire-a-Husband, that company you see around town. Are you married, Ranger Saunders?"

He chuckled. "No. I haven't had that experience yet."

"After interviewing me, you must be thankful."

"Not every marriage ends in pain—I'm sorry. That sounds incredibly insensitive."

"Not at all."

She watched him dry his hands as he turned to her. "Before any more time passes, I want you to save my cell number in your contacts. If an emergency arises, you can call me any hour of the day or night."

"Thank you," she answered. She retrieved her phone and entered the number he gave her. "Now, will you tell me why you're having me watched?"

His hands went to his hips. "Did you know that LifeSpan fired your husband a month ago?"

"No," she whispered then sank down on the nearest chair. "That would have been after we separated. He never told me." She buried her face in her hands. "What happened?"

"LifeSpan has been losing money. One of the other accountants under your husband started checking back and discovered payments made to a company he could find no record for. They were payments your husband authorized. A full investigation has been started. They're still tracing back to see how long it had been going on. So far they've found over nine-million dollars missing since the beginning of his employment with them."

Natalie gasped. "Rod did that?" She simply couldn't believe it.

"Yes, but the only portion of that money to show up in his personal records was four-hundred thousand."

Her head lifted. "He always wanted to keep our bank accounts separate. It's all making sense now. Four-hundred thousand?"

"Your husband withdrew it from his checking account the day before he was killed, and I'm guessing that whoever trashed your house wanted to get their hands on it."

She shook her head. "We've never had that kind of money, not even with our combined salaries." Her body trembled. "I've been living with a monster."

"It's evident he's been a disturbed man most of his life. I'll learn more when I speak to his grandmother. Though her husband died recently, I understand she's still alive and was able to give the police a few facts about Park. I need to question her."

Natalie's incredulous gaze met his. "That means Amy has a great-grandmother! I can't fathom it. They have to have been in pain for years wondering what had happened to their grandson after he escaped."

"I'm sure that's true. One day soon we'll get all the answers. Will you be available to talk some more tomorrow? Since it'll be Sunday, morning or afternoon will be fine for me."

He was coming by again? Her pulse picked up speed for no reason. "Do you want to come over at eleven or so? Amy will be ready to go down for her nap around then."

"Eleven it is." He walked through to the living room and looked out the front window. "The surveillance team is parked out front in a carpet-cleaning truck. They'll keep an eye on you around the clock to make certain you're safe. I'll see myself out the back door."

She watched his tall, rock-hard physique slip out through the kitchen and disappear from view once he reached the neighbor's yard. Natalie clung to the open door. He'd convinced her that she and Amy could be in danger, but as shocking as all the revelations had been, he'd had a calming effect and she felt confident she wasn't alone in this horror story.

KIT PHONED THE surveillance team from his truck to give them instructions. Once he let them know he was leaving the premises, he drove to the freeway and headed for Marble Falls. He'd have to drive fast to be on time for his mother.

Needing to talk, he used voice commands to dial Cy, a fellow Ranger who was working on another case. He was gratified when he heard his friend's voice over the speakers.

"Hey, Kit. I saw you in TJ's office earlier. What's going on?"

"I've been given a case the captain doesn't want anyone else to know about yet, but I'd like your advice."

"You don't need anyone's advice."

Kit made a strange sound in his throat. "I think I do."

"Where are you?"

"Headed for the rodeo in Marble Falls. Brandon's competing tonight."

"He's racking up great times so far."

"Let's hope he can keep it up. He wants to win that championship in the worst way."

"My bet is on him. Kellie and I are planning to join you for the Las Vegas trip in December. So, what's going on? What did you want to ask me?"

"How did the boss take it when you told him you were going to go undercover as Kellie's husband?"

A long silence followed. "Don't tell me you're planning to do the same thing with this new case?"

Kit exhaled a sigh. "You've just answered my question."

"No—forget what I said. Tell me about the case."

"The wife of the guy who was found dead in his hotel room a week ago could be in serious trouble—someone broke into her house today. But having a surveillance crew watching her could scare off the bad guys. I want to catch them in the act. I'm thinking about posing as her cousin who is taking his retreat from the parish he serves to be with her for the next week."

"A *priest*?"

"Yeah. I'll wear a collar."

Cy made a funny choking sound. "Have you told the widow what you've planned?"

"Nope. I wanted to run it by you first. If you think my plan holds water, then I'll tell the captain. If he gives his approval, then I'll talk to her."

"What haven't you told me yet?"

"Get ready for an earful."

In the next few minutes Kit had revealed everything to his friend, including the fact that the widow had a sixteen-month-old daughter. When he'd finished, a loud whistle came from the other end of the line.

"Harold Park has been on the FBI's Most Wanted list for years! You mean to tell me his wife didn't have a clue?"

"As far as I can tell, not one."

"Maybe she's as big a con artist as he was."

"No. When she saw the rap sheet, she went white as a ghost. I followed her to the bathroom and watched while she lost her lunch. That kind of reaction couldn't have been faked.

"Seriously, Cy, I would have treated this like a normal case until Detective Carr called me about the burglary.

"If you could have seen her house, you'd know that whoever is after the money isn't going to stop. My hunch is that the money he embezzled over the years has been laundered, but he kept four-hundred thousand for quick cash. Someone knew he had it and came to the house hoping to find it stashed there. But they only had that short window of time. I'm afraid they'll be back for a more thorough search. That puts Mrs. Harris and her daughter at risk and changes the way I planned to go about solving the case."

"I hear you. Knowing what I know now, your priest idea sounds inspired. It makes sense that a family member would stay for a while to help her in her time of grief. The collar will stop any gossip, especially if she's attractive."

Kit didn't comment.

"Is she?"

"Is she what?"

"Attractive."

"Yes."

Cy waited for his friend to continue. "Just yes?"

"Yes. Just *yes*!"

"Whoa! For you to clam up like this means she must really be a knockout. Right?"

"That's not what's important here."

"The hell it isn't! I've been there, remember?"

"I do remember. Vividly. That's why I called you." Cy had ended up marrying the woman he'd been protecting.

"You shouldn't have any trouble with the captain. No matter how you do it, he knows Kit Saunders always gets his man. But he'll give you the same advice he gave me. Be careful you don't cross the line."

Kit knew exactly what his friend meant. A strong attraction could complicate a case while you were trying to remain professional. "That won't happen to me. This woman's in shock."

"So was Kellie. But it wore off. When it wears off for Mrs. Harris, that's the time to worry."

"Thanks for the warning, Cy," he muttered. "Give my best to Kellie. Talk to you later."

He ended the call and dialed TJ. Might as well run it by him. Depending on the captain's answer, Kit would have some preparations to make before eleven in the morning when he saw *her* again. He'd have to keep his head down and try to concentrate on his work instead of those eyes, green as lush spring grass.

NATALIE HAD ALREADY used up a week of her ten-day paid leave for family bereavement. She was thankful for a few more days to play with her golden-haired daughter before going back to work.

She was just the sweetest little thing, Natalie thought, as Amy ambled around the house on fairly steady legs, pushing her little grocery cart. Natalie adored her and sang her favorite songs over and over again while she got her dressed and fed her breakfast.

One day Amy would have to know about her father, but that time wouldn't come for years yet. Since he hadn't been around at all since moving to the hotel, she rarely said "dada." Her vocabulary consisted of about twenty words. She loved her farm animals and had *cow* and *pig* down pat. Amy particularly loved the "Eensy Weensy Spider" song and always said the word *spout* very loudly when the time came.

At quarter to eleven Natalie let Amy drink her milk from a sippy cup then put her down for a nap and sang nursery rhymes until the toddler's eyelids fluttered closed. After tiptoeing from the bedroom, Natalie walked back to the kitchen to clean off the high chair and straighten up. The Ranger would be arriving in a few minutes.

She hurried into the bathroom to give her hair a brush-through and put on some lipstick. Today she'd dressed in a blue-and-white print blouse with jeans and sandals. When her cell rang, she went to her bedroom where she'd left it on the bedside table.

She knew when she saw that there was no name on the Caller ID that it had to be him. Miles. The two hang-up calls had come in on her landline. She clicked Answer. Maybe he wouldn't be coming, after all. "Hello?"

"Mrs. Harris? Ranger Saunders here. How are you this morning?"

The vibrancy of his deep voice curled through her. "I'm fine, thank you."

"If I didn't know better, I'd believe you. I'll be by in a minute. I'll be driving a dark red Altima and I'll come to the front door this time. You mentioned putting your little girl down for a nap—I'll knock so I don't disturb her."

"That's very considerate of you. I'll listen for your knock."

"All right, then." He clicked off.

Natalie left her bedroom and paused at the nursery door. She'd played hard with Amy and figured she'd stay asleep for an hour, but probably no longer. By that time, presumably, the Ranger would have finished whatever it was he needed to do and gone.

The news had been shocking enough when she'd learned that Rod had been found shot. But whatever news the Ranger still had to share couldn't possibly be as ghastly as what she'd learned about her husband yesterday. *He'd committed murder.*

Rod hadn't even been his name… She shuddered to think that she'd been married to him all that time. *They'd had a baby together.* Natalie felt violated. She hadn't slept well.

She was still deep in torturous thought when she reached the living room and heard a soft knock. As she opened the door, another shock awaited her. The Ranger who'd left her home yesterday had been so transformed she almost didn't recognize him except for those fabulous hazel eyes and dark brown hair.

Standing in front of her was a tall, well-honed priest carrying a suitcase. He wore a traditional, short-sleeved, tab-collared clergy shirt in a vivid blue color and a pair of black pants. His white collar stood in contrast with the tan of his complexion, and even more brilliant was his smile. It took her breath.

"If you'll invite me in, I'll explain."

Natalie had been staring at him. His remark caused the blood to rush to her face. She opened the door wider so he could pass.

He put the suitcase down on the floor in the small entry hall before following her into the living room. "Your daughter is asleep?"

She nodded. "Please sit down. Can I offer you coffee or a soda?"

"Nothing for me, thanks." This time he opted for the couch while she chose the same chair as before.

"Once in a while we get a case that requires full-time watch to protect an endangered party. After talking to my captain, I see two ways to go about handling your case. We can continue to guard you with a surveillance crew outside your house 24/7 or you can have someone living with you on the inside."

Her pulse started to race. "When you say someone, do you mean *you*?"

"That's right. How would you feel if your fictitious cousin Todd Segal from Wyoming spent his retreat from his parish here, to help you through your bereavement for the next week or so? The choice is yours, of course, but I'd prefer to protect you myself."

The gorgeous Ranger was resourceful, too. She was awed. "I have to admit you look the part." Inwardly she was shaken by the idea of his living in her home.

"Good." His lips twitched. "Being a priest who happens to be your only living relative, aside from your absentee father, won't raise any eyebrows. Those who know your situation will be happy you have someone from the clergy who is family and looking after you since losing your husband. I'll be able to protect you while I carry out the investigation."

Natalie couldn't sit still and got up from the chair. "You think that inmate who escaped with Rod is after the money, don't you?"

He studied her features. "I only mentioned him in passing. After eight years, anything's possible. We have no idea what new contacts Rod's made in that time. I've barely scratched the surface of this investigation. How soon do you plan to go back to work, by the way?"

"On Wednesday."

"That'll have to change, I'm afraid. Until the culprit is caught, it's not safe for your little girl to be left with your friend. This person might resort to kidnapping to get the money."

The color drained from Natalie's face but the Ranger quickly continued.

"Since we don't want any harm to come to you or your daughter, it makes the most sense for you to stay home and take care of her until we know it's safe for you to go back to work. This is an emergency situation. My boss will make the arrangements with Mr. Willard at the pharmacy so your position isn't jeopardized while you take more time off."

Natalie could hardly keep up. She was reeling. "Thank you for that."

"The sooner we can get this case solved, the sooner you can get back to the life you've made for yourself. While you're home, we can work more quickly."

We? "What can I do to help?"

"I need to know your husband's habits, his friends. I'll be going through your personal accounts and phone records. Did he have a laptop?"

"Yes, but he took it with him."

"It wasn't found at the hotel, but the police impounded his car. Maybe it will have turned up there, along with his cell phone. I'll find out when I get the forensics report. Have you gotten rid of any clothes and belongings he may have left here?"

"He only left a few things behind. I don't want anything he owned. I don't even want to see it. Whatever was found at the hotel can be donated or thrown out."

"I'll let them know. As for his things here, we can go through them together. You might recognize clues that wouldn't make sense to anyone else. I guess the crucial question is…would you be uncomfortable with me staying here for a while? Will it make your daughter unhappy? If the answer is yes to either of those questions, then I'll have you watched and proceed on my own."

Everything was happening so fast she could barely

process it. Natalie put her hands in the back pockets of her jeans. "I can tell you'd prefer working from here."

"I would. I came dressed for the part, just in case." He sensed her hesitation. "But please don't let that sway you. We'll get the job done either way."

He seemed decent up front. She didn't know why, especially given the way Rod had deceived her, but she trusted him even though they hardly knew each other. "I want this menace gone from my life as soon as possible. I have confidence in you."

"Thank you for that. My gut tells me the person who ransacked your house isn't finished, and if I'm here 'round the clock I may be able to speed up the process of catching him. But you have to be absolutely comfortable with the decision."

She'd been pacing the floor but came to a standstill. With her own personal Texas Ranger guarding her and Amy day and night, what was there to be worried about? "I *am* comfortable with it," she stated quietly, "but I don't have an extra bedroom."

"That's not a problem. I have a bedroll out in the car. I can put it down anywhere. Hopefully, I won't prove too much of an inconvenience."

"If there's any inconvenience, it will be my daughter waking you up in the middle of the night when she starts crying. It doesn't happen very often, but I'm warning you now her lungs are in perfect working order."

His half smile melted her insides.

"While she's asleep I'll go out to the car and bring in my bedroll and groceries."

"Groceries?

"I told you I came prepared. I stopped at the store on the way here. I'll put my things in the den, out of sight."

He'd thought of everything, she marveled. "Let me give you the second remote for the garage so you can pull your car in. I've got an extra house key for you, too. I asked Rod to give them back to me when he left for good."

"Thank you." He followed her into the kitchen where she started searching through a drawer.

"How soon do you think the police will release his car?"

"I'll find out tomorrow."

"I only ask because the baby quilt I made for Amy is missing. I can't think why it would be in his car, but it's the only place I haven't looked. We only ever went places as a family in my car. He said his was for business only."

"Everything they found when it was impounded will be returned to you."

She nodded and handed him the key chain with the remote.

"Be right back."

SO FAR, SO GOOD.

Kit walked outside, aware the surveillance team was still parked a little ways down the street. He phoned them and told them they could leave, but he wanted them back at six-thirty in the morning.

After activating the remote, he drove into the straightened-up garage and then pulled Natalie's car inside, next to the laundry room door. He got out and made a first trip into the house with the groceries.

While she put the items away, he went back for his tool bag and suitcase. He took his things to the den with its floor-to-ceiling bookcase on one wall. The entertainment center took up the other wall. He noticed more framed pictures on the end tables; pictures of Natalie with a woman he guessed must be her mother.

He could see where Natalie Harris got her beauty. And the barefoot little girl in a ruffled, lemon-colored top and shorts who now came into the den with one of her push toys had the look of both of them. She stopped short of bumping into Kit's shoe and looked up at him with her grayish-green eyes.

Was she about to cry at seeing a stranger? It didn't even matter—Kit decided she was the cutest little girl he'd ever seen.

Natalie had come into the den and leaned down to address her daughter. "Amy? This is Ranger Saunders. He's going to stay with us for a while."

"Ranger Saunders is too hard to say. You can call me Kit."

Surprised, Natalie stood. "Kit? I thought you said your name was Miles."

"It is, but most people call me Kit. It's my nickname." He hunkered down next to Amy. "Hi, honey. What's your name?"

"Tell him you're called Amy," her mother urged. "You can say it. Ay-mee."

"Me," her daughter mimicked, leaving out the *A*.

He smiled and pointed to his chest. "I'm Kit. Kit."

"You can tell her mind is working on it," Natalie murmured.

"Kit," the little girl finally pronounced.

"Yes." He nodded, pleased she'd picked it up so quickly. "I'm Kit, and you're Amy. Now what's that toy you're pushing?"

She immediately started moving it around, showing him she understood.

"That makes a fun noise," he said, encouraging her.

Pretty soon she'd circled the room. When she looked to see his reaction and smiled, it tugged on his emotions.

"Cow," she said and ran out of the den on her sturdy legs.

Natalie eyed him in amusement. "She's gone for her favorite animal in her toy box."

While they exchanged a silent glance, Amy came back clutching the brown-and-white-spotted plush cow in her hand. She toddled over to Kit, almost stumbling, and held it up. "Cow."

"That's right. It's a cow." Kit took it. "Moo."

"Moo-oo," she repeated with all the earnestness in her then hurried out of the den.

"Oh, Kit. I'm sorry. Now that she's got a captive audience in you she's going to bring you all her farm animals."

"I'm not complaining." He sat on the couch and put the cow on the coffee table. Before long the golden-haired cherub returned and handed him a purple pig. "What's this?" he asked her.

"Pig!"

Her enthusiasm caused him to burst into laughter. "That's a colorful pig. What sound does it make?"

Amy tried to imitate the oink. He couldn't believe she was so adorable.

"Oink, oink," he grunted. Her giggle delighted him. "You're without a doubt the cutest, smartest little girl on the planet. That's because you've got a terrific mother." Though her father had been a criminal, he'd done one thing right in his life to have helped create this angel.

"Come on, sweetie." Natalie swept her up in her arms. "Let's go out to the kitchen and give you a little snack."

Kit followed them, enjoying the interplay between mother and daughter. After Amy had been put in her high chair, Natalie fastened a bib around her neck. Then she sliced half a banana into small pieces and put them on the tray. He took a seat at the table to watch while the little girl took her time eating each mouthful of the fruit.

He glanced at Natalie. "Since you weren't expecting a guest to stay with you, I thought I'd fix us some lunch with the groceries I bought. How does that sound?"

"I was just going to ask if you'd like a sandwich."

"Sounds good, but I'll do it."

She smiled, but he didn't know what else was on her mind because her cell phone rang, reminding him of the reason he was here.

"Go ahead and answer it, but put it on speaker."

Her smile faded before she reached for the phone and checked the Caller ID. "It's Jillian."

"Good. Let her know a cousin is visiting you and you won't be going to work for a while, so you won't be needing her services. The less she knows, the better."

"I agree." Her voice trembled. She clicked on. "Jillian—"

"Hi. I just want to know if you're okay."

"I'm much better today."

"That's good. You sound better. I saw a car in your driveway earlier. If you have company, call me when you have time to talk."

"It's all right, I have time now. I was going to call you today, anyway. My cousin Todd is here from Wyoming for a few days, so I'm taking more time off of work and won't be needing you to look after Amy next week."

"Oh. Okay… I'm glad you have family with you."

"Me, too. Thank you for everything you've done for me, Jillian. I'm hoping life can get back to normal soon."

"I hope so, too. Take care, Natalie."

"You, too. I'll call you soon."

"Okay. 'Bye."

She'd done well. The plan was in place.

Chapter Three

Natalie disconnected and turned to Kit, who was making sandwiches. "Jillian knows there's a lot I haven't told her."

"But you told her enough so she won't be planning on babysitting for you next week. This way she and her daughter will be safe."

"Thank heaven for that. If anything were to happen to her because of Rod…"

"It won't. That's why I've taken precautions."

While he assembled cold cuts and cheese, she reached for a paper towel and got busy cleaning up the pieces of banana Amy had thrown on the floor. Natalie darted the Ranger a look of frustration. "A week in my house and you'll find that half her food doesn't make it to her mouth. If you have any little nieces or nephews, you know what I mean."

"Not yet. My brother, Brandon, is a professional steer wrestler—he's headed for the championship competition in Las Vegas in December, as a matter of fact. One day he'll settle down and have a family."

"How old is he?"

"Twenty-eight. Two years younger than I am. This will be his last year on the circuit."

"How exciting! Are you a rodeo fan, too?"

"I used to be a steer wrestler myself. We took turns being wrestler and hazer for a long time. But I quit when I went into law enforcement."

"From steer wrestler to Ranger. Both put your life at risk."

He studied her features. "Have you ever been to a rodeo?"

"Many times while I was in college. Remember my friend in Phoenix? She used to be a barrel racer. We rode horses on her parents' property and it was fantastic to watch her speed around the barrels. I tried it, but I was a complete failure. She taught me about the various events. Steer wrestling is incredibly dangerous."

"But you liked it?"

"I loved it all!"

Kit was enjoying their conversation so much he almost forgot he should be working on her case. Talk about crossing the line. Already he was getting too close to it.

Within ten minutes they sat eating lunch while Natalie fed Amy some Cheerios. Kit chuckled to watch her tease her daughter. She'd move her hand around and Amy's little mouth would follow, open in anticipation.

"Tell me something, Natalie. Has Amy ever ridden on a jet?"

Her eyes widened. "No."

"What would you think if we took her for her first ride tomorrow morning to Denver? I need to talk to

Rod's grandmother in person. The detective said she's been told her grandson passed away. Seeing Amy would do her a world of good and could jog her memory. I'm hoping she'll be able to give me some background information about his teenage years that might help me fit some of the pieces of the puzzle together."

Natalie's face lit up. "If she was a loving grandmother, then I know she'd be thrilled to see her great-grandchild. I could take some pictures of them together for Amy's baby book."

Kit was pleased with her reaction. "I'll make the arrangements. It's less than a two-hour flight. We won't have to be there long."

"I thought about her last night…Rod's grandmother. What's her name?"

"Gladys Thomas Park."

"He never said a word about a living relative. The poor thing lost a married son and a grandson. How cruel life can be…" Her voice trailed off.

"All the more reason for us to go there and surprise her. In the meantime, where will you be the most comfortable to answer some more questions?"

"The living room. Amy will bring her trove of treasures from the nursery and stay busy going back and forth for another few hours."

He got up and cleared the table while she wiped Amy's hands and face and got her down from her high chair. When she told him she'd finish up, Kit went to the den for his suitcase. He took it to the bathroom and swapped his clerical shirt for a casual sport shirt.

Any time he needed to answer the door, he'd quickly put it back on.

When he returned to the living room, Natalie and Amy looked up from the floor where they were working on a puzzle. They made a beautiful sight. Both pairs of eyes wandered over him. "So my cousin is on vacation from the priesthood this afternoon?"

"Yup. It's Ranger Saunders reporting for duty. If you're ready to get started, I'll turn on the digital recorder." She nodded and he proceeded. "First question. Your income taxes. Where do you keep a copy?"

"Rod prepared them at work and kept everything there."

"Then I'll have to speak to the people at LifeSpan. Did he have the Sentra when he met you?"

"Yes. He said he'd bought it three years earlier."

"From a dealership here in Austin?"

"I don't know."

"Did he continue making monthly payments on it?" Amy toddled over to give him a horse from her farm collection. "Thank you, honey." She smiled and got busy again.

"No. Rod said he'd paid it off."

"Do you know where he kept the title?"

"At the office with everything else. You've probably never met a wife so in the dark about her husband's dealings. It never occurred to me not to trust him. I've been so naive, I'm embarrassed and ashamed."

He grimaced. Harold Park had put her on a short leash. He sat forward in the chair and handed Amy a dog she'd dropped. He made a barking sound she tried to imitate before handing him a goat. "There's no shame in trusting someone."

Natalie looked up at him. "My mother never trusted my father and always questioned him about everything. They had a lot of fights. At twelve I was old enough to understand their marriage wasn't happy. I swore that if I ever got married, I would never do that to my husband. If she were still alive, I'd ask her to forgive me.

"After what's happened to me, I'm thinking my father must have done something to ruin their marriage from the beginning, but Mom tried to shield me from the worst of it. She didn't believe in divorce. Thank heaven, she didn't live long enough to find out I married a true, hardened criminal. Mother and daughter both lucked out, didn't we?"

Kit took a deep breath. "Bad marriages happen to wonderful people. Tell me about the early days before Amy came along. What did you do? Did you take trips, go out a lot? Did you make friends with other couples? Did he have a favorite sport or hobby? I'm trying to get a picture of the pattern of your lives."

The answers to those questions and many others— How much time did he spend away from home? Did he take the occasional business trip? Was he an early riser? Did he get home from work late? If so, how often? Did she go to his work once in a while? Which people at work did he associate with?—took up the rest of the day. Natalie's observations led Kit to realize Harold Park had been the worst kind of controlling husband.

By nightfall Natalie had fed Amy dinner and now

whisked her off for her bath. Kit took advantage of the time alone to prepare for the trip and make half a dozen phone calls to get his investigation started.

Their flight to Denver was booked for eight fifteen. It meant they'd have to be at the airport by six thirty. Kit hadn't been on a trip since April when he'd flown to Billings, Montana, to watch his brother compete at the Wrangler Rodeo Competition.

Natalie peeked into the den to say good-night. Kit looked up from the desk. "We'll need to leave the house at six."

"We'll be ready."

"I've already taken the liberty of putting Amy's car seat in the back of my car. When we reach the airport, it will go on the plane with us. Technically, Amy qualifies as a lap baby, but I want her secured no matter what. In Denver we'll install it in the rental car."

"Thank you for taking care of that. I've been wondering how it was all going to work. Don't stay up too long. Good night, Kit."

"Good night, Mrs. Harris."

"Please call me Natalie."

He nodded.

Once she'd vanished, he walked through the house to make sure windows and doors were locked. When he finally stretched out on the floor of the den in his sleeping bag, Kit rolled onto his side. He'd put his .357-caliber SIG Sauer halfway under his pillow, very much hoping he wouldn't have to use it while he stayed here. Natalie was living through a horror story with her daughter and didn't need anything else to add to her pain.

He was determined to solve this case as soon as possible because already he could tell he was emotionally involved to a greater degree than he should be.

"Be careful not to cross the line," Cy had warned him.

Unfortunately that advice had come too late. In truth Kit found himself looking forward to tomorrow with more excitement than the occasion warranted.

AT 11:00 A.M. they entered the Cottonwood Nursing Home in downtown Denver. Amy had sat on Natalie's lap for most of the flight, but she seemed happy enough to be held by the Ranger as they spoke to the people at the front desk. Everywhere they went, whether it was the tourists on the plane or the staff here, people stared at the fabulous-looking, dark-haired priest holding Natalie's little golden girl.

"Father Segal? If you'll go down the hall and around the corner on the left, you'll find Gladys Park in room 120. She's had bouts of pneumonia that have weakened her. This is the best time of day to visit. Once she's had lunch, she usually sleeps and it's difficult to wake her."

As they walked along, Natalie got a good feeling about the clean, nicely decorated facility. If Gladys's care was as good, that was the most important thing. When they reached her door, they found it open. The ninety-two-year-old woman was in bed with the head raised. She was listening to the radio.

Kit nodded to Natalie. "Go ahead and talk to her while I hold Amy."

Her heart pounded extra hard as she walked over to the side of the bed. She'd already made up her mind to keep certain facts to herself to be kind. The woman's eyes were closed. "Gladys?"

"Yes," she responded without opening them.

"My name is Natalie. I've come to visit you."

"That's nice."

"I used to know your grandson Harold."

A long silence ensued before the woman turned her head toward Natalie. "You knew Harold?"

"Yes. I was married to him. We live in Austin, Texas."

That revelation caused her eyes to open. "Come closer. My eyes aren't what they used to be."

Natalie leaned toward her. "Can you see me better?"

"A little. What's your name?"

"Natalie."

"You married Harold? When?"

"Two and a half years ago."

"I haven't seen him since he was sixteen. He went to prison. He must be thirty-three now."

"He passed away last week," she said gently. "Of complications from an infection. But we have a daughter, sixteen months old. Her name is Amy. Would you like to see her?"

Gladys tried to lift her head off the pillow but she was too frail and feeble. "You brought my great-granddaughter to see me?"

Tears filled Natalie's eyes. "I did. My cousin, Father

Segal, came with us." She looked over her shoulder at Kit who moved toward her. She reached for Amy.

"Can you see her?"

"Bring her closer."

Natalie leaned in close with her little girl. "Amy, this is your great-grandmother Gladys."

The older woman lifted her hand to touch Amy's. "Oh…my precious girl. I wish I could see better, but I have glaucoma." In the background Kit was taking pictures of the three of them with his phone.

"She's golden blond and has gray-green eyes."

"Harold had gray eyes like his mother. His parents were killed in a car crash you know."

"Yes. Harold told me."

"We did what we could for him, but he was inconsolable. I think something happened inside his head. When he got older, he got mean and kept running away. We didn't know what to do to help him. I didn't know he'd been released from prison. I'm glad he met someone like you after all those terrible years. You sound so kind."

"Natalie is a very kind woman, Mrs. Park," Kit interjected. Natalie moved far enough away so Kit could lean toward Gladys.

"Who are you?"

"I'm Natalie's cousin. She wanted you to meet your great-granddaughter before any more time passed. We flew here from Austin with Amy."

Tears trickled out of the corners of the older woman's eyes. "My prayers have been answered."

"What prayers were those?" His question was so tender, the sound of his tone pierced Natalie's heart.

"That I would hear some news of our grandson. Now that you've brought my great-granddaughter to see me and let me know Harold has gone to heaven, I can die knowing he met a wonderful woman and had a baby."

While the older woman wept, Natalie buried her wet face in Amy's hair.

"Is there anything I can do for you, Gladys?" Kit asked.

"Did you know Harold?"

"No," he answered. "Tell me about him."

"He was a beautiful-looking boy and a good child."

"Did he have good friends?"

"Not after he changed. There was one boy he ran around with. They got into trouble all the time."

"Do you remember his name?"

"Salter. Jimmy Salter. I'll never forget him. His parents couldn't do anything with him, either. My husband and I felt like such failures…you can't imagine."

"What did your husband do for a living?" Natalie interjected.

"He was an architect for a firm here in Denver. We had hopes our son might be an architect one day." Her voice faded.

"In his last years of freedom Harold became an accountant."

"Harold? An accountant? Oh, my. He hated school."

"Which high school did he attend?" Kit asked.

"Tabor High."

"Did you work when you were a young, married

woman?" Natalie discovered she wanted to know everything this woman could tell her.

"Oh." She gave a half laugh. "I taught girls' physical education at Tabor High for thirty-eight years. I used to run marathons. Now I can't make this body work anymore."

"Amy runs constantly. I think she might have inherited that trait from you."

Natalie's gaze swerved to Kit's. Streams of unspoken thoughts ran between them. "Do you have friends who visit?"

"Oh, yes. People from our church. I've been well looked after. My husband saw to that. But we couldn't do anything for our Harold." She wept again.

"Yes, you did," Natalie contradicted her. "You gave him a wonderful home after his parents died. No one could have done more, but I'm sure you're tired now. I'll come to visit you again soon and bring Amy. I want her to get to know you."

There was no more talk. They'd worn her out. Natalie held Amy until her little girl started to squirm to get down. Kit must have seen the signs and plucked her out of Natalie's arms. Gladys had gone to sleep.

With tacit agreement they left the room and walked down the hall to the reception area. Kit approached the desk. "We had a nice visit with Gladys and can see she's well taken care of. We'll come again soon."

"She'll love that."

Natalie left her name and phone number in case they needed to call her. Then she joined Kit and they left the nursing home for the rental car.

Kit got behind the wheel. "What do you say we stop at a drive-through for lunch and go to a park for a little while before we have to head to the airport? It'll give Amy a chance to run around."

"That's a wonderful idea."

Before long they located a nearby park. They found a nice spot for their picnic and Natalie laid Amy down on a quilt to change her diaper. With that accomplished, she disposed of it in the diaper bag then sanitized her hands.

Kit opened the sacks. Natalie fed Amy some yogurt with fruit. She ate part of Natalie's grilled-cheese sandwich while Kit tucked into a ham-and-cheese melt. They drank soda and laughed at Amy's antics as she walked around on unsteady legs in the grass, carrying her cow. It went everywhere with her.

"I don't think I fooled Gladys. She had to have known he'd escaped from prison and was a fugitive. I'm just thankful she didn't press me."

Kit eyed her thoughtfully. "In my opinion she was so thrilled you gave her news about Harold and let her see her great-granddaughter, she was willing to go with what you told her."

"She's a lovely, bright woman. So was her husband. It means—"

"It means Harold's parents were great people, too," he interrupted her. "Something *did* go wrong inside his brain. It's tragic, but it happens. Are you glad we came?"

"Oh, yes, Kit. Thank you for making it happen. I've learned so much…the kinds of things I'll be happy to tell Amy about when she's older. But what about you? Do you think the name of that former friend of his could give you a lead?"

"I'm counting on it, but I'll look into it tomorrow. Tonight I'd like you to call your friend in Phoenix and ask her when would be a good time for a visit. We'll fly out there. The sooner the better. Wednesday if we could."

Natalie felt a fluttering in her chest. "I'll call her after nine when she's off work."

"Good. I need to talk to her in person. Her answers could prove crucial to this case."

Natalie waited until Amy drank the fresh milk she'd poured into her sippy cup. "All right, young lady, it's time to get you back to the car."

Time to bring an end to this amazing day with Kit Saunders, Texas Ranger *extraordinaire* in every sense of the word. In three days Natalie's life had undergone a drastic change. She could tell she wasn't the same person who'd walked into her house on Saturday to find it violated the way Rod had violated her. The life she'd had with him seemed light-years away.

TUESDAY MORNING KIT was up and out of the house early. He left a note for Natalie that he needed to get to headquarters and that a surveillance team in a television-repair van was parked near the house to keep watch over her until he got back.

He'd dressed in his clerical shirt and headed for the office. Before he did anything else, he needed to talk to his boss. Everyone who saw him walking down the hallway did a double-take before he reached the captain's inner sanctum and knocked on his partially open door.

"Come in."

Kit did as he was told. "TJ?"

The gray-haired man looked up and gave Kit the once-over. "I thought I'd seen it all. Don't get any ideas about changing careers, *Father* Saunders. We need you around here."

"Thanks." Relieved to find his boss in a good mood, Kit sat.

"Give me an update."

After five minutes TJ had been brought up to speed. "What's your next move?"

"I'll be in my office for a while. I've got to check out the information on Jimmy Salter. After that I'll touch base with Forensics. Tomorrow I plan to fly to Phoenix. Mrs. Harris's friend may hold the key to the person who killed Harold Park."

TJ regarded him shrewdly. "I take it you've cleared Mrs. Harris as a suspect?"

"I'm one-hundred-percent certain she's innocent of everything except falling in love with an expert con man."

"Are you taking her with you again?"

"Yes. I believe her friend will be more comfortable with Mrs. Harris there."

"What about the toddler?"

Just thinking about the little girl put a smile on Kit's face. "Amy will be coming, too. I don't want her separated from her mother."

"So it's Amy now." TJ looked amused.

Kit could see where this conversation was headed and got to his feet. "I won't take up any more of your time."

"Watch your back. Let me know if you need more help."

"Thanks, TJ."

Once he'd settled at his desk, Kit made two calls to Denver. The first was to the school board to request information on Jimmy Salter and his family from their records. His second call was to the police in Denver to have them search their files for a rap sheet on a Jimmy Salter. Thanks to Mrs. Park he had approximate dates to go on.

With that accomplished he called Forensics. Stan, the lead forensics expert, invited him to come downstairs to discuss what he knew at this point in the case.

Before he could leave, his cell rang. He saw Natalie's name and his pulse sped up. Maybe she'd reached her friend. "Hi."

"Hi. You told me to phone if I got one of those hangup calls. It just happened."

Kit checked his watch. It was ten to ten. "I'll get someone on it immediately. That's three so far, right?"

"Yes. The two last week and now this one."

"Okay. Did you reach your friend?"

"My call went to Colette's voice mail. I asked her to call me back ASAP."

"Then I'm sure she will. I'll be here awhile if anything else comes up. How's Amy?"

"Running around as usual with toys in both hands."

He chuckled. "See you later."

On the way down the hall Kit almost collided with his friend Luckey, who grinned. "Well, well. Do I call you *Monsignor*?"

"It's Father Segal."

"On you it actually looks believable. Cy told me you've gone undercover on the Harris case and she's really hot."

"I didn't say a word about her."

"That's why Cy figured it out. Where's the fire?"

"I'll tell you later."

"I want to know chapter and verse. If you need backup, I'm available."

"Thanks. I just might need you."

Kit hurried past him and took the stairs two at a time to reach the bottom floor where the forensics department was located. Once through the doors he stopped at the office of another colleague. Rafe.

The man smiled. "The collar looks good on you, Kit."

"Thanks."

"What can I do for you?"

"Check on the call that went to the Rodney Harris home maybe five, six minutes ago." He wrote down the number of Natalie's landline. "I need to know who made it, anything you can."

"Will do."

"I'll be in with Stan when you've got any information for me."

He moved on and found Stan comparing pictures

on a screen. "Stan? Have you got prints from the Harris home yet?"

"We're still working on them, but we have the prints off Harris's cell and laptop. There were several different sets on and inside the car. They found a couple of long black hairs on the front passenger seat. We're running the prints that aren't Harris's or his wife's through the AFIS database. I'll email you a copy of the results." He eyed Kit but didn't remark on the collar.

"Great."

"Les has finished going over the car. It was totally clean. By that I mean there wasn't anything in the glove compartment, no litter. Nothing."

"When he checked the spare tire, did he see anything that could give us a clue where the car was serviced or purchased?"

"No. He found the laptop and cell phone in the trunk. They found a thumb print on the lid and we're looking at it now. The two items were wrapped in a baby quilt, of all things."

"Obviously it was wrapped to hide it from view."

"You'll notice two hundred and eighty thousand miles on the car."

Interesting. Why would an accountant have done so much driving? "Later in the day someone from the staff will drive it over to Mrs. Harris's house with the deceased's personal effects."

"Thanks, Stan."

Kit would look through everything with her later. He hoped Natalie could remember how many miles were on the car when she'd first met her husband. If he had a travel allowance, Kit knew the mileage on the car would be way over the limit.

"Kit?" He turned to see Rafe coming toward him.

"What did you find?"

"That call originated from a throw-away phone."

"I thought so. Appreciate it."

Whoever had broken into Natalie's house was anxious to get back in. Maybe the culprit thought the money had been stashed in the attic, unless he'd checked it out the first time. Kit phoned Stan.

"Kit?"

"One more question. Did the forensics team take prints on the trap door leading to the attic at the Harris residence?"

"Let me check." He came back on the phone quickly. "No."

"Okay. Thanks."

Forensics should have checked that. Kit would do it after he went back to Natalie's house. Now that he was through here, he'd head over to LifeSpan Pharmaceutical and get the status on the investigation of the accounts fraud.

When he reached the car in the underground parking, he removed his clerical shirt and put on the brown Western shirt he'd brought, the badge attached to the front pocket. Then he phoned Natalie.

"Hi. I just found out Rod's car will be delivered to your house later today. They'll phone you first. I just wanted you to know what to expect. You'll be happy to learn that the baby quilt you made was found in the trunk."

"Oh—I'm so glad. I hated losing it. Thanks for letting me know."

"Of course. While I have you on the phone, do you have any idea of the mileage on Rod's car when you first started going out with him?"

After a silence she said, "No. Like I said, I simply wasn't that curious. Sorry."

"Not a problem. See you later."

But before he could put his key in the ignition, his cell rang. After a glance at the Caller ID he answered.

"Brandon? What are you doing calling me at this time of day? I thought you'd be out practicing with Scott!" He always liked talking with his brother.

"You're not going to believe what happened. Scott was in an accident this morning and went to the hospital with a broken leg."

"You can't be serious." Kit's eyes closed tightly. His brother had just lost his hazer for at least three months. The timing couldn't be worse considering his schedule on the rodeo circuit. "How did it happen?"

"A semi's brakes failed and it T-boned Scott's Silverado before it ended up in a field. It was a miracle no one was killed, but Janie's a wreck." Brandon sounded shaken.

"I'm sure she is." He ran a hand through his hair. "What hospital is he in?"

"Seton."

Kit would have to give Scott a call.

"I don't know what to do, bro. We have a competition coming up this Saturday night in San Antonio. I've got to find another hazer, but that takes time."

"Ask Whitey. He's worked with you before."

"I'm afraid he's off his game these days."

That meant Whitey was drinking again. "Try Pete."

"He's not up to speed anymore."

"Then spread the word you need a hazer fast!"

"I'm sure I'll find one, but not in time for Saturday night."

Kit had too much on his mind to give his brother's problem a lot of thought. "Can you afford to give this rodeo a miss while you search for someone else?"

"I guess I might have to."

Kit heard the disappointment in his voice.

"Kit?"

He could hear it coming. "Yes?"

"Are you working on a big case these days?"

"Yup. In fact I'm in the middle of it right now and I have to go. I'll call you later when I get a chance." He rang off and headed across town. It didn't surprise him that his phone rang again as he pulled into the guest parking lot at the LifeSpan Pharmaceuticals.

He clicked on. "Hi, Mom. I heard the news."

"It's a darn shame, Kit."

"I agree."

"But Brandon was counting on winning in San Antonio. Is there any way you could haze for him on Saturday night? You know better than anyone how important it is, and there's no one better on a horse than you."

That's right, Mom. Butter me up to make me feel guilty.

"I'm working undercover on a big murder case. It's

possible I might have to be in Arizona this weekend."
Natalie and Amy would be with him. He found he
didn't want anything to get in the way of his plans. "If
I can see a way to do it, I'll call him, but don't count
on it."

Though his mother didn't say a word and never
would, he could hear her thoughts.

*Your father never put his Ranger duties ahead of
his family when it counted.*

And that hurt.

Chapter Four

Natalie was in the middle of making tacos for dinner when she heard her cell ring. There was no Caller ID, but Kit had given her a heads-up earlier in the day. "Hello?"

"Mrs. Harris? I've brought your husband's car home. It's in the driveway with the key in the ignition. I've left it unlocked."

"Thank you so much."

"You're welcome."

After she hung up, she turned to Amy who was in her playpen chewing on one of her doughnut toys. "I'll be right back, sweetie."

She left the kitchen and hurried through the house to the front door. When she opened it, she found it strange to see Rod's Sentra again, knowing he was out of their lives permanently. Her feelings were so dead where he was concerned, she felt as if she'd turned into an entirely different person.

She opened the trunk and reached inside for the quilt. The cell phone and laptop were in there, too. She gathered everything in her arms and shut the trunk before rushing back into the house.

Natalie put the things down on the couch but carried the quilt to the kitchen. "Look what I've got, honey!"

Amy pointed at it, but kept playing with her red doughnut. While she was still content, Natalie took the quilt to the laundry room to be run through a wash and dry cycle. Before doing anything else, she walked to her bedroom and gathered the rest of Rod's things from her closet. Kit had mentioned wanting to look through them, so she carried them to couch.

Once he'd checked everything, she would throw out the last vestiges of Harold Park. A shudder ran through her body. She couldn't wait to be rid of anything that reminded her of him. That included his car. She'd take it to a used-car dealer to sell or, better yet, donate it.

While she finished cutting up some tomatoes and avocado, her cell rang. She saw that it was Colette and took the call.

"Oh, Colette. Thanks so much for calling me back."

"Of course. I feel terrible that I couldn't fly to Austin for the graveside service, but Chad had his appendix removed that morning and I had to stay home with him."

"I understand totally. To be honest I'm glad you didn't come." Natalie's voice shook.

"What's wrong?"

"Do you have a few minutes?"

"Sure I do."

Natalie gave her friend a brief account of what had happened.

"My gosh, Natalie. I don't believe it. Rod was a felon?"

"Afraid so. There's so much to tell you, but not right now. The reason I'm calling is because the Texas Ranger who's working on the case wants to fly to Phoenix to talk to you about the day you saw Rod with that other woman."

"You mean the woman who wasn't your cousin?"

"That's the one. When would it be okay to come? He says the sooner the better. Amy and I will fly there with him."

"Come tomorrow. Chad is feeling better every day. I'll meet you at the airport to save you time."

"That would be wonderful! I'll tell him and get back to you on the exact time."

"Good. I'll wait for your call. Stay safe."

"With a Texas Ranger guarding us, I'm not worried. Talk to you later."

No sooner had she hung up than the phone rang again. She picked up and said hello.

"Hi, Natalie." Kit's deep voice resonated through her. "I'm almost to the house. I don't want you to be alarmed when I let myself in."

"Thank you." He was so considerate, she was amazed. "Just so you know, Rod's car is out in the driveway. The key is still in the ignition."

"In that case I'll park his car in front so I can drive into the garage."

"I'd like to get rid of it, maybe through a donation if I can." The words rushed out of her, revealing her state of mind.

"Forensics is done with it, so you're free to do whatever you want."

"I still haven't found the title."

"Don't worry about it. You can donate without one."

Relief swept through her. "That's good. I have news for you. Colette called and said we can fly to Phoenix any time tomorrow. She's offered to meet us at the airport."

"That's terrific news. I'll see you in a minute."

Natalie lifted Amy and put her in the high chair with one of her toys. Then she folded up the playpen and put it back in the nursery. Before long she heard the garage door lift. To know he would be there in a minute made her excited, and it had nothing to do with the fact that his job as a Ranger was to keep her safe while he solved this case.

In a very short time she'd gotten use to this temporary arrangement and had made dinner with him in mind. *Remember it's only temporary, Natalie.* But try telling her heart that when he appeared in the kitchen wearing the clerical shirt. There was no way to shut out his arresting masculine appeal.

"Something smells good."

"Are you hungry?"

"Famished."

"I've made tacos."

"Give me a minute and I'll join the two of you. Here's the key to Rod's car."

When he disappeared, she got out a jar of junior sweet potatoes and lamb for Amy. Kit walked in a few minutes later wearing a claret-colored polo shirt and jeans. It was getting harder and harder to keep her eyes off him.

"Help yourself to anything you want, Kit."

His smile made her pulse race. "Since you're busy feeding the cherub, can I fix you a plate, too?"

"I'd love it."

She'd fried half a dozen tortillas. One taco was enough for her. But when she saw that he'd eaten four filled shells along with a large helping of tossed salad, she wondered whether she'd made enough.

He finally sat back in the chair and centered his hazel gaze on her. "That was delicious."

"I can make more."

"If I take another bite, I won't have room for the chocolate-marshmallow ice cream I bought."

Natalie grinned. "So that's your favorite dessert?"

"One of them. I'll get it. Would you like some, too?"

"Sounds good."

"Do you think Amy would like a taste?"

"Of course, but she's not getting the chance yet. Once she discovers chocolate, all my hopes of feeding her healthy foods will go right out the window."

Laughter rumbled out of him, grabbing the little girl's attention.

"Kit—" Amy spoke his name with a happy smile.

"That's my name, sweetheart." The tender look he gave her daughter touched Natalie deeply.

Kit dished out two bowls of the ice cream and handed one to Natalie.

She took a mouthful. "This is yummy. I haven't had this flavor in years."

His dessert disappeared in a hurry. "I've loved it since I was a little kid."

"What else did you love as a boy?"

"Oh…the usual. Snakes, fireworks, anything scary or that went boom."

A chuckle escaped her lips. "Your poor mom."

"Yup. With two sons to raise, she had her hands full while Dad was out on a case."

Her head lifted. "A case? What kind? What did he do?"

He eyed her through narrowed lids. "He was a Texas Ranger."

"Was?"

"Dad was killed in a shootout when I was seventeen."

"Oh, no—I'm so sorry." She bit her lip. "How hard to have lost him that early in life. I'm surprised it didn't put you off becoming a Ranger."

He shook his head. "Just the opposite. In 1842 Sam Houston got a law passed that provided for a company of mounted men to act as Rangers under Captain John Coffee 'Jack' Hays. My ancestor was one of them."

"You're serious?"

"Yup. Three of the other Rangers who are my close friends are also descendants from the original company. The guys at headquarters have nicknamed us the Sons of the 40."

"Wait a minute. I saw the four of you on TV. You brought down that huge drug ring!"

He nodded.

"I thought I'd seen you before." She studied his rugged features. "I guess it isn't all that surprising that you wanted to be like your father. The Texas Rangers are legendary and honorable. The kind of men any child would look up to."

"That described Dad."

Natalie thought of her own father. Those adjectives didn't apply to him.

"Captain Hays and his company of forty defeated the Comanche raid at Bandera Pass, protecting the southern and western portions of the Texas frontier. Their story was passed down through my father's side of the family. I knew that one day I wanted to be a Ranger, too."

"I guess with a heritage like that, you couldn't help but want to follow in your father's footsteps."

"Something like that. Throughout high school and college I did steer wrestling, but it couldn't last. So I quit to go to the police academy. Eventually I was taken on as a Ranger."

"Amy and I are very thankful you did," Natalie said in a quiet voice and got up to clear the table. Much longer and she'd be begging to hear the rest of his life story.

He'd told her he was single. Much as she wanted to know, she didn't dare come out and ask if he was romantically involved with someone. It was none of her business.

"I left Rod's things on the couch with his laptop and cell phone. If you want to go through them, I'll do the dishes and give Amy her bath before putting her down."

"Thank you for dinner. I didn't stop for lunch. You

have no idea how happy I was to smell your food cooking."

She laughed. "As long as I'm staying home, plan on eating any or all of your meals here. It's nice to have someone to cook for." Natalie could have bitten her tongue off for saying that, but it was too late.

An hour later she walked into the living room having put Amy to bed for the night. She found Kit searching through the files on Rod's computer.

"Have you discovered anything that could help you?"

"No. He was too savvy to leave clues behind. I've been through his clothes, but they're several years old and nothing stands out. If you'll notice, he removed the labels so it would be difficult to trace where they'd been purchased." Kit stood. "Do you mind if I bring in the step ladder from the garage? I want to look for prints on the attic lid and climb inside to take a look around."

The attic? "Go right ahead." She'd almost forgotten the house had one.

"I'll be as quiet as I can."

Natalie didn't doubt it. So far he seemed to be an expert at everything he did. While he put on plastic gloves and got busy, she went to the kitchen for a garbage bag to put Rod's old clothes in to take to Goodwill.

To her shock Kit came down the ladder carrying a medium-size suitcase. His gaze flicked to hers. "Have you ever been up in the attic?"

"Never."

"Have you ever seen this suitcase?"

She shook her head.

"Let's see what's inside." Natalie followed him into the kitchen and he put the case on the table. "It's locked, but I have tools." He went to the guest bathroom for his bag. She marveled that within seconds he'd opened the lock.

When he lifted the lid, she gasped.

"Well, well. Two firearms. Both .45-caliber Colt automatics," he muttered and picked them up one at a time. "They're loaded, ready to go."

Natalie's hand covered her mouth. The police had been to her house but they hadn't been in the attic.

"Now we know at least one item the intruder was looking for. It's clear your husband knew this person and gave him a key to get into the house. Since Rod was killed before this person could find out where the guns were hidden, it makes me think there was a third party involved in all this."

"Anyone that desperate should have realized the attic was the perfect place to hide them," Natalie commented. Certainly she hadn't thought of it. But Kit wasn't like other people. He had the instincts only a few men were blessed with. That's why he was a Texas Ranger.

"Maybe he was afraid you'd get back from the funeral before he could search the attic and be found in the act." He shot her a piercing glance. "Thank God, you didn't go in the house when you saw the state of the garage. If that person had still been in there, he could have taken you hostage."

Or worse.

Natalie weaved in place and grabbed the back of a chair for support.

Kit closed the suitcase. "I'll take this to Forensics in the morning. Excuse me while I put the ladder away."

When he came back into the kitchen, he removed the gloves and tossed them in the trash. "Let's go sit in the living room." He motioned for her to lead the way and she settled into an armchair. He went to the den for his laptop before sitting on the couch.

"I spent most of the afternoon at LifeSpan and discovered how your husband was cheating the company. Right around the time he started working for them seven years ago, he set up a dummy corporation that looked like any of the dozens of companies LifeSpan pays for their services. But, of course, it didn't perform a service.

"The money went straight to a bank where it was deposited into a falsified account. He made constant withdrawals and pocketed the money under another of his assumed names."

Natalie was scandalized. "What did he do with it?"

"It's my guess he invested it in various ventures—real estate, maybe—under yet another alias to hide what he was doing. The point is, the auditor who worked under your husband couldn't understand why the offsite, independent auditor hadn't caught the problem years ago."

"That's horrible."

"Agreed. He stole millions from the company. It seems likely to me your husband bribed an independent auditor to go into business with him and paid him a percentage for looking the other way. Or that person was a criminal like Rod. Your husband was fired a month ago when the independent auditor couldn't be found to substantiate Rod's claims that he'd done nothing wrong. The FBI is staging a full investigation."

She stirred restlessly. "I hope that money can be recovered and given back to LifeSpan."

"I could wish for the same thing, but my main concern right now is to keep you safe until we know who invaded your home and the culprit is arrested. Let's hope your friend in Phoenix has some information that can help. Give me a minute to make the reservation."

Kit pulled out his cell phone and got to work and it didn't take him long before he was tucking it back in his pocket. "I have to take the guns to the lab, so we'll drop them off on the way to the airport. Our US Air flight will leave at eight-thirty and put us in Phoenix by ten-ten. That means we'll have to leave here by 6:15 a.m. Does that work for you?"

She nodded. "Amy's already asleep. I'll get everything packed and be ready."

"Good. Do you mind if I do some wash right now? The clerical shirt is drip dry, so there's no problem."

"Of course, I don't mind, but I can do it for you."

"Thanks, but no. I've fended for myself for years. To be surprised with a dinner you fixed was a treat I didn't expect."

"In that case I'll phone Colette right now."

While he gathered his things to take to the laundry room, she called her friend and gave her the time and terminal. "One more thing, Colette. The Ranger will be dressed in a blue shirt with a collar, like a priest."

"You're kidding—"

"It's a long story. I'll tell you the details after we get there. If anyone should ask, he's my cousin, Father Todd Segal."

"Natalie—"

"I know it sounds bizarre, but he's saving my life, literally."

"I believe you. See you tomorrow morning. Do I dare tell you I can't wait to meet him? A real Texas Ranger?"

"Yeah. I'm still having trouble taking it all in."

"What's he like?"

Natalie wasn't going there. "He's the personification of the perfect Ranger."

"I get it. Code for gorgeous, right?"

Right. Something had to be wrong with her to be talking like a high school girl to Colette when she was in the middle of a grave situation that could cost more lives.

"I'll see you tomorrow, Colette."

She hung up, afraid to say anything else because Kit had come back into the living room. Natalie looked up at him. "I'm going to go pack a suitcase for Amy and me, and then get to bed so I can wake up in time for our flight."

He nodded. "Get a good sleep. While we're gone tomorrow, another surveillance team will watch the house."

"Kit?" she said in a tremulous voice, getting to her feet.

"What is it?"

"Thank you for everything you're doing. I'm so grateful I don't know how I'll ever be able to repay you."

"This is my job, Natalie."

"I know, but you've helped me get through one of the darkest periods of my life. You've restored my faith in the idea that there are good men out there, although probably not many as exceptional as you. Good night."

NATALIE'S WORDS CAUSED Kit's throat to swell. For the first time since working as a Ranger, Kit had become personally involved in a case. He had no business caring about her or her daughter except on a professional basis, but it had happened, anyway. If he were honest with himself, he could admit to a strong physical attraction to her at the cemetery before they'd even met. It was the kind of chemistry that couldn't be explained.

The only thing to do from here on out was to focus on the case and cut out all ideas of spending unnecessary time with her, such as watching a movie together before they went to bed. *Concentrate, Saunders, or you're in big trouble.*

He turned out lights, secured the doors and got ready for bed. He still wasn't ready to sleep so he checked for new messages on his laptop. The response from the police in Denver sparked his interest first and he opened it to find the rap sheet on Jeremy Roos Salter. So he *was* in the criminal database!

Jeremy Roos Salter, 33. Born: Denver, Colorado. Home address: Lima Street. Aliases: Jessie James, Walter James, Sal Jameson. Currently serving a life sentence at Atwater Federal Penitentiary, Northern California, for arson, aggravated assault and the murder of two police officers. Incarcerated seven years ago.

That meant Harold and Jeremy could have been committing crimes all through their teens before the law caught had up with them. The visit to Gladys Park had produced a big lead for Kit. He intended to fly to California to have a talk with Salter.

While he was still up he called Information to find out if there were any Salters living in Denver. There were quite a few, but none on Lima. Tomorrow he'd phone every listing. Maybe he'd stumble across someone related to Jeremy or who could tell him something about the family that once lived on that street.

Stan had sent him a message saying the thumbprint found on the lid of the laptop had been sent to the criminal database because it hadn't matched Mrs. Harris's prints or her husband's. He'd requested that the results be sent to Kit ASAP, and Kit was anxious to see them.

One last item of business before he quit for the night. He reached for his cell and texted his brother.

No time to call hospital. Give Scott my condolences. Won't be in Texas this weekend. Hope you find a hazer fast. Kit.

He put down his phone and closed his laptop, refusing to feel guilty. For years he'd watched out for Brandon, but this was one time his duty to work came first. But a nagging little voice reminded him it wasn't all duty, not where Natalie was concerned. Not by a long shot.

"THERE'S COLETTE. SHE'S wearing the yellow blouse and cowboy boots," Natalie said as they walked off the plane into Terminal Four on Wednesday morning.

Her friend's long, chestnut-brown hair rippled as she hurried toward them and hugged both Natalie and the baby. "It's so good to see you."

"I feel the same. Colette, meet my cousin, Father Segal."

Colette smiled at Kit and shook his hand. "I'm so glad to meet you, Father. I'm thrilled you're helping Natalie through this difficult time."

"It's my pleasure."

"Since I know you're in a hurry, I thought we'd go up to the third level and have a meal in the restaurant. They have high chairs. Maybe Amy will let me hold her after we're seated."

"I'm sure she will."

"Let's go."

Kit followed the women, carrying the diaper bag and car seat. The restaurant Colette had chosen was the perfect place for an interview.

Once they'd ordered lunch Natalie excused herself and took Amy to the restroom where she could change her diaper. Kit handed her the bag.

His eyes lingered on her retreating figure, dressed in a peach-colored top and jeans that outlined the soft curve of her hips. With those long legs and that honey-blond hair, he was sure every male in the place must be watching her progress.

The reason he was there at all suddenly dawned on him and he switched his gaze to Natalie's friend. "I appreciate your being able to meet us here, especially since I hear your husband is still recovering from an operation."

"I'd do anything for Natalie and my husband is much better—he plans to go to work tomorrow. I just hope I can help you."

"Whatever you can tell me about the woman you saw with Rod Harris will be useful. I'll be recording our conversation." She nodded. "Could you describe her physically for me?"

"She couldn't have been more than five-two, five-three. She had a small frame, maybe a hundred and ten pounds."

"What about her hairstyle?"

"Dramatic. Her hair was long and black. She had it swept around back and coiled near the top of her head with a clip. She had dark brown eyes."

"Race?"

"Her coloring made think she was Hispanic."

"Did she speak with an accent?"

"No, not that I noticed."

The waitress arrived with their food and, after she excused herself, Kit resumed his questioning. "How was she dressed?"

"Very stylish. A designer-type dress and high heels. She went a little heavy on the makeup. You're probably surprised I noticed so much, but it was because she was so striking, almost like a fashion model. Rod said she was Natalie's cousin, but I found that surprising because I'd never heard about her."

"I wish all the witnesses I interrogated had your memory. Did he introduce her by name?"

"He said something like Myra or Mara, but he was in a hurry and I didn't quite catch it."

"That's fine."

"I wish I'd been more observant," Colette murmured. "Now that I know the truth, I guess he just wanted to get her out of there as fast as he could."

"I'm sure of it. Did she have a suitcase with her? Maybe a tag that would identify where she'd come from or where she was going?"

"Not that I recall. I was in a hurry myself."

Kit nodded. "How did he treat her? Like a friend or a lover?"

"I didn't pick up on anything more than that they knew each other."

"Do you remember the car he was driving?"

Colette frowned. "I think he was standing next to a white car, but I can't be positive."

"Good," he said as Natalie returned and put Amy in the high chair. The little girl pointed to him. "Kit."

"Hi, sweetheart." He put a cracker on the tray for her.

Natalie's friend broke into a smile. "She knows you."

"She catches on fast." He smiled back.

"Amy has her mother's smarts. One day I hope to have a baby as adorable as this one."

"I'm sure you will." Natalie's spring green eyes darted to Kit. "Sorry I was gone so long. The place was crowded. Forgive me if I'm interrupting you."

His gaze played over her. "There's nothing to forgive. I've already asked all my questions pertaining to the case. Colette here has a keen eye—she remembered details I wouldn't have expected. It helps immensely."

The three adults started to eat their lunches and Amy munched happily on her crackers. Kit addressed Natalie's old friend.

"Tell me about your barrel riding days, Colette. Do you still compete at the rodeo?"

"Not anymore. Sounds like Natalie has been telling tales out of school."

"That's because you were an excellent barrel racer," Natalie countered. "And guess what? Kit—I mean, *Father Segal*'s brother is a steer wrestler. In fact he's competing at Nationals in Las Vegas in December."

Colette's eyes lit up. "What's his name?"

"Brandon Saunders from the Lazy S Ranch in Marble Falls, Texas."

"Father Segal used to compete in the same event," Natalie interjected.

"Really. How come you're not still riding?"

"My career forced me to give it up."

"That happened to me, too. Those were the good old days. I'll have to keep an eye on your brother's numbers. When is his next event?"

"Saturday night in San Antonio, but I don't know how he'll do because he lost his hazer this week."

Natalie's smile faded. "What happened?"

"His hazer, Scott, was in a car accident and has a broken leg. Brandon's got to find a replacement, fast."

Colette finished the last of her sandwich. "Good ones are hard to come by. That's bad luck. I feel sorry for both of them. Hazers are almost invisible unless they make a mistake, but a bull dogger couldn't get a low score without an outstanding one to keep that steer close."

Her comment made Kit feel even guiltier.

She looked at Natalie. "How soon is your return flight?"

"In an hour. We'll go downstairs in a few minutes. Amy has almost finished."

Natalie had been feeding her a jar of chicken and stars. Kit couldn't get over what a great little traveler she was.

"In that case I'm going to leave you two in time to get some grocery shopping done before I drive home." She rose and hugged the baby and Natalie. Then she turned to Kit. "It's been a pleasure meeting you, Father Segal."

He got to his feet. "Thank you for getting together on such short notice. Your testimony is more helpful than you know. If you think of anything else, don't hesitate to call me on my cell. Here's my card." He handed it to her.

"I promise." She started to dig through her purse but Kit shook his head. "This lunch is on me. Drive safely."

"I will." Her glance rested on Natalie. "We'll talk soon."

"I'll call you. Thank you again."

Colette made her exit and Natalie wiped Amy's face and hands, then turned to Kit. "We're ready to go downstairs. Amy's been awake since first thing this morning, so I think she'll probably nap most of the way home."

"She's been a model child—honors go to her mother."

"I can't take the credit. She came this way."

Kit decided not to argue. But he'd watched how Natalie handled her daughter and could tell she was a terrific parent.

He left money for the bill on the table, picked up the bag and car seat, and ushered the girls out of the restaurant, anxious to get back to Austin. It pleased him that he and Natalie would be going home together. He found himself enjoying her company more than he should.

His thoughts returned to the case. Stan should be getting back to him with the rest of the information on the fingerprints. He was also eager for the FBI agent to send him the background on the missing independent auditor for LifeSpan. As for the black hairs found in Rod's car, they might be a match for the hair on the woman Colette had seen with Park. She could be an unsuspecting girlfriend or she might be an accomplice, corrupt to the crown of her head.

There was a lot Kit needed to go through and analyze. But he decided that while he was waiting for more answers, he would fly to California in the morning and speak to Salter. Hopefully he could get it all in and be home by tomorrow night. He couldn't get this case solved fast enough.

Chapter Five

After a homemade spaghetti dinner, Natalie gave Amy her bath and put her down for the night. She'd grown restless on the airplane and hadn't napped the way Natalie had hoped. Kit had taken over and held her for a while, playing with her toes. Amy had loved it when Kit pointed to each toe; laughed each time he touched one. The stimulation had kept her awake, but happy. Now what she needed was a good night's sleep.

Natalie found Kit in the den, laptop open while he talked business on the phone. He saw her and motioned for her to come in. She sat in one of the comfortable armchairs, pleasantly tired. It had been great to see Colette again, but their visit had been too brief.

"How's the cherub?" Kit asked when he finished his call.

"Out like a light."

"I'm not surprised. Your little girl has done enough flying for a while."

"She's never had a more exciting week in her life. A new man in the house, jet-plane rides—"

His eyes studied her for a moment. "It makes me happy that she doesn't mind having me around."

"Mind? She's crazy about you. It astonished Colette when Amy said your name in the restaurant."

He flashed her a smile that turned her heart over. "That made my day. Thanks for flying to Arizona with me. I wanted your friend to feel comfortable."

"I enjoyed seeing her again, even if it was only for an hour. Was she really able to help you, or were you just saying that to be polite?"

"Anything but. It was well worth the trip. Now I need to find a pattern using the evidence I've gathered, but that means I have to fly out again tomorrow morning. I'll be going alone this time."

"Are you able to tell me where?"

"California. I'm going to interrogate Jimmy Salter at the federal prison."

"You mean Rod's—childhood friend went to prison, too?"

"Afraid so. He killed two police officers."

"I can't believe it." Natalie looked at Kit. "How long will you be gone?"

"I could be home by tomorrow night, but probably the next day. Since Salter is a lifer, you never know about getting him to talk. He might cooperate and tell me something important about Harold.

"Then again, he could refuse to speak. But when I tell him your husband was murdered, it may jar him into revealing a critical piece of information I could use. But don't be concerned. You'll be watched at all times while I'm away. They'll follow you if you want to drive to the store or whatever."

"I know that." She averted her eyes. "I just don't see how you can stand to face a cold-blooded killer."

"It's part of my job."

"I know, but it's so awful."

"The satisfaction of capturing a dangerous criminal makes it all worth it."

Natalie lifted her head. "You're an amazing man."

"Like I told you before, my childhood was filled with snakes and things that go bump in the night." Kit's half smile didn't dispel her concern for him.

"Do you ever have nightmares?" she asked.

"I've had my share, but not because of my career. The one that returns on occasion has to do with letting my father down."

Natalie swallowed hard. "Was he a demanding man?"

"Not at all. He was kind and straight as an arrow. I thought he was next to perfect."

"Well if I had a chance to meet him, I'd tell him the size of your footsteps match his." The second she'd spoken, heat swarmed her cheeks.

Kit's gaze held hers. "When I have that nightmare again, I'll remember your words."

Natalie stood from her chair. "If you've got to make an early morning flight, I'll say good-night."

"Once I've installed a camera over the front door, I'll call it a night, too."

The man was doing everything possible to keep her

safe. "Is there anything I can get you before I go to bed? There's still some iced tea left over from dinner."

"No, thanks. It was delicious, but if I want any more, I'll get it."

You heard him, Natalie.

She turned and retreated through the house to her bedroom. But after she got into bed, she couldn't fall asleep. She shouldn't be upset because he had to leave for a day or two to carry out his job. And it wasn't because she was afraid for him. That wasn't the problem.

Something else had happened to her; something she could never have imagined. Natalie's attraction to Kit had grown roots. How was that possible in so short a time?

To get him off her mind, she reached for the remote and turned on the TV on the dresser.

The next thing she knew, she was waking up to a Thursday morning news show. She shut it off and got out of bed.

After throwing on a robe Natalie walked down the hall to the nursery. Amy was still sleeping. When she reached the den, she saw Kit's sleeping bag rolled up and propped in the corner. Her watch said eight-fifteen. He'd gone.

She moved to the living room and looked out the window. A van marked Kitchen Remodels was parked a few houses down. To be watched over made her feel secure, but she felt an emptiness because—

Oh, stop it, Natalie.

Upset with her herself, she took a shower, washed her hair and got ready for the day in shorts and a sleeveless blouse. Amy was up and playing in her bed when Natalie entered the nursery.

"Good morning, my little love."

Her daughter answered her with a smile and some baby chatter. Once she'd had a diaper change and Natalie had found her a cute little sunsuit to wear, they ate breakfast. While Natalie was feeding her, Amy said Kit's name.

"Kit's not here, honey." So her daughter was missing him, too. Things just weren't the same today.

Before it got too hot, she grabbed her cell and took Amy out back, setting her in her playpen on the patio with some toys. Natalie started the mower and cut the small back lawn, then moved the little kiddie pool off the patio and onto the grass.

It was filled with plastic ducks and geese. Amy loved to throw the beach ball into it, then climb in and throw it back out, along with the ducks. Later Natalie would put a little water in so Amy could splash.

While the little girl toddled around the yard, Natalie lay on the lounger to watch. The emptiness she'd felt earlier hadn't gone away. Resigned to be in this condition until Kit came back, she returned a series of calls to people who'd left messages.

Once that was done, she phoned Information and got a number for car donations for veterans and was pleased to discover that a towing company could collect the Sentra before the end of the day and would leave her a receipt. Relieved to have taken care of that so easily, she turned on the hose and put some water in the pool.

Amy loved it and they played until it was time for

lunch. At nap time, Natalie brought in the mail then cut the grass out front. With Austin on water restriction, the sprinklers went on at four in the morning at her address on Wednesdays only. The lawn didn't look that great, but it couldn't be helped.

The last thing on her list was to put the key to Rod's car back in the ignition. Just as she finished and came back into the house, her cell rang. She looked at the Caller ID and clicked on.

"Colette?"

"I hope it's all right to talk for a few minutes."

"Of course."

"Is the Ranger still there?"

Natalie gripped the phone tighter. "No. He's away. Probably until tomorrow."

"I'm alone, too. Chad has gone to work for a few hours and I've taken today off in case he doesn't feel well and comes home early. To be honest, he was going crazy around here and driving me crazy too. I've decided that husbands make horrible patients. Anyway, I just had to call you and—"

"I know what you're going to say," Natalie interrupted. "Yes I find him terribly attractive and wonderful, but he'll wrap up this case soon and that will be the end of it."

"Want to make a bet? I saw the way he looked at you when you took Amy to the restroom." Natalie's heart pounded. "I hope he's not married."

"He's not."

"That's good, because no priest or married man should watch a woman the way he watched you."

"Don't be ridiculous." Natalie was afraid to believe it.

"I'd say it's a good thing Father Segal isn't really a priest because from where I was sitting, he was already in big trouble."

"Colette—"

"It's true, and you had the same expression in your eyes when you looked at him. What's great is that Amy likes him, too."

"She does. This morning she noticed he wasn't here and called out his name."

"See?"

"See what?" Natalie asked with impatience.

"If you're honest with yourself, you'll admit that you fell out of love early in your marriage. It's about time you met someone else. And, Natalie, I have to tell you that Ranger Saunders is fantastic with a capital *F*."

Colette never minced words. She attacked head-on. That was one of the reasons Natalie loved her friend so much. "I agree with you," she said in a shaky voice. "But I don't dare read anything into what's going on. He's never given me even a hint that he might be interested."

"It's there in his eyes and in his body language."

"I think you're imagining things because you want me to be happy."

"I do want you to be happy, but only with the right man."

"Thank you for being the greatest friend in the world."

"Ditto. Keep me posted about what's going on. Call me anytime if you need to."

"I will. You're the best, Colette. 'Bye for now."

Amy slept on, so Natalie looked around for something else to do. She threw out two of the flower arrangements that had died, wishing they could have lasted longer. People had been so kind to her she decided to write thank-you notes. It would keep her from thinking about Kit, out interrogating a killer.

Her day wore on and by the time she and Amy were eating their dinner, the tow truck driver had come to the door to give her the receipt for the car. She watched through the screen as Rod's car was hauled away. She was relieved to know the surveillance team was keeping watch. Tomorrow she'd take the bag of his clothes to Goodwill and that would be the end of any physical reminders. *Except* for photographs.

Those were in a scrapbook Natalie had put away on a shelf. One day Amy would want to see pictures of her father. Natalie hoped that by the time Amy started asking questions about her daddy, enough years would have gone by that she'd be able to deal with them.

After Amy's bath, she put her to bed and was just coming out of the nursery when her phone rang. She hurried to the kitchen, hoping it might be Kit, but when she checked the screen, it listed an area code and number for Denver. With a frown, she answered.

"Hello?"

"Is this Mrs. Harris?"

"Yes."

"This is Mrs. Issac, the director at the Cottonwood Nursing Home. You asked that we contact you about Gladys Park. I'm sorry to have to tell you that she died in her sleep this evening." Natalie gasped. "She was comfortable to the end. There'll be a little memorial service here for her on Monday at noon. Her close friend and her pastor are arranging it, but I knew you'd want to be notified."

"Thank you so much for letting me know. It means the world to me. I don't think I can make it to the service, but I'll have flowers sent."

"That would be lovely."

Natalie disconnected and buried her face in her hands. Another death. Emotion overwhelmed her and she broke down sobbing.

BEFORE KIT PULLED into the driveway, he waved off the surveillance team. With his business concluded early, he'd taken the next flight out of San Francisco.

He drove into the garage and went into the house, where he found Natalie in the kitchen, crying her heart out.

"Natalie?"

She lifted her tear-streaked face. "You're back—" she cried in surprise. "Oh, Kit, I'm so glad you're here."

Without thinking, he pulled her into his arms and held her while she wept. "What's happened?" he asked. His lips brushed her silky blond hair.

"G-Gladys died this evening. I got the call a few minutes ago."

He gathered her tighter.

"What if you hadn't arranged for us to fly to Denver when you did? I would never have known her. Thank heaven you took pictures while we were there. Amy will cherish those when she gets older." Natalie lifted her head so their mouths were only inches apart. "If it weren't for you, I don't know how I would have gotten through everything. I owe you so much."

Kit kissed the tears on her cheek but eased her away from him, even though it was the last thing he wanted to do. "I'm glad we went, too. Come on. Let's go in the living room and talk. I take it Amy is down for the night."

She nodded and led the way.

He waited until she sank onto a chair before settling in at one end of the couch. "When is her service?"

"Monday. At the nursing home. I told the director I couldn't be there, but I'd send flowers." She wiped her eyes with the backs of her hands. "How did your prison visit go?"

"Salter was uncooperative, but I spoke to several other inmates. One of them told me he knew the forger who'd made fake IDs for Salter and some of the other prisoners. The name was Barni Esger. It could turn out to be a promising lead if I can find a connection between this person and Rod's forged documents."

"Where is this forger?"

"He's serving time in federal prison at Leavenworth in Kansas."

She groaned. "All those men in prison… That means you'll be taking another trip."

"Yes."

She lowered her head. "Did you tell Salter that Rod had been killed?"

"I did. He showed no emotion, which isn't surprising." He eyed her for a moment. "I saw that the Sentra is gone."

"I took care of it today and donated it to the veterans."

"That would have been my choice, too. How's Amy?"

"She said your name at breakfast. She was looking for you."

He'd missed both of them. Kit wasn't supposed to develop attachments, but there were a lot of things that weren't supposed to have happened since he'd met her. Such as putting his arms around her to comfort her. It had felt so right.

"If you're hungry, there's plenty of food in the fridge."

"I ate on the plane, thanks. Any more hang-up calls?"

"No. It's been quiet. I'm glad you're back safely. I know you have work to do, so I'll say good-night."

Keep your mind on the case, Saunders. "See you in the morning."

After she disappeared, he went to the den and opened his laptop. Another response from the criminal database. Neither of the two guns had been fired recently, and any prints had been wiped clean. The thumbprint on Park's laptop had turned up a mug shot of a female. She'd been arrested for possession of drugs and petit larceny eight years ago in Denver, Colorado.

The same time as Harold Park.

The woman had been charged with a misdemeanor and was jailed for eighteen months.

He scrolled down.

Juanita Morales, alias Myra King, Mara Fletcher, Myrna Foyle. Female, 24, 120 pounds, 5'3". Blond hair, blue eyes.

Kit's head reared in reaction. He'd hit the jackpot! Juanita had to be the sister or wife of Alonzo Morales, the convict who'd escaped with Harold. Assuming she'd dyed her hair and worn colored lenses eight years ago, this could very well be the woman Colette had seen at the airport with Natalie's husband.

He scanned a copy of the rap sheet and emailed it to Colette. He'd like to hear what she had to say about the mug shot. He also wanted to know the precise location where she'd seen them in the airport parking area. Tomorrow he'd get one of the guys at headquarters to go through the airport security tapes for footage of Harold and his companion.

After he'd sent the message to Colette, he read through his other emails. The rest of the prints from the house and car matched those of Harold Park and Natalie Harris. Nothing surprising there.

He'd suspected all along there was a third party involved in this case. Linking Juanita to Alonzo made the most sense. Juanita was probably the one who'd provided the transportation to drive the two fugitives out of state during their escape. Everything had been planned. Which one of them had ransacked Natalie's home?

Together they'd picked LifeSpan to defraud, but they would have needed all kinds of fake ID and forged documents to make it happen.

With his mind racing ahead, he suddenly realized his cell was ringing. He reached for it and recognized the Arizona number. "Is this Colette?"

"Yes! I saw the image you sent me and didn't want to keep you waiting. *She's* the woman I met! The coloring is different, obviously, and she's lost a little weight since that photo, but I saw her up close and those are her exact features."

"That's all I needed to hear. Your information is going to help me solve this case."

"I hope that's true. You asked where I ran into them. It was in the short-term east parking with access to the Jeppesen Terminal on level four, kind of in the middle."

"That will help us locate the right security cameras. Thank you for calling me back."

"Of course. I can tell Natalie is in the best of hands. Good luck, Ranger Saunders."

After he'd hung up he emailed headquarters and asked that a team pull the tapes. He'd take a look at the footage after his return from Kansas.

With that sent, he checked the front door camera, pleased to see that no one had come to the door but the man from the towing service.

Content that all was well for the moment, he locked up the house and got ready for bed. It was a long shot to fly to Leavenworth tomorrow, but he intended to build this case with as much evidence as possible. He'd been supplied with a rap sheet on Barni Esger, and while he might not have any reason to cooperate, Kit had to try.

Before his arrest, the Dane who'd immigrated to Colorado with his father when he was a teen, had been a professional photographer celebrated for his scenes of the Colorado mountains. For years he'd used his studio in Fort Collins, Colorado, to cover up his real work of producing fake credentials for dozens of hardened criminals throughout the country.

Despite what Kit's instincts told him, he had no proof that Esger had been involved. But any information he could get out of the man would be valuable. For Harold to obtain an accounting job with LifeSpan in the first place, he'd have had to reinvent his whole life. He'd fooled so many people for so many years. The Morales duo, too. Had Esger set them up with fake documents, as well?

One of them had killed Harold. Kit was sure of it. Had they discovered he'd double-crossed them? Had they turned on him because that had been their plan in the first place? Who knew the ins and outs of their ménage à trois? He'd like to lock them both up for good.

Kit was looking forward to the day when Natalie was safe and could put all this behind her.

When he climbed into his sleeping bag, he imagined being curled up with her. She always smelled delicious. What a loving heart she had, crying over Rod's grandmother. He admired her immensely for the way she was handling the horror of having been married to a criminal.

Another woman might have fallen apart, but not Natalie. Her strength of character was awesome to witness as she carried on with her life for the sake of her daughter.

Amy was a little angel. He'd never felt an attachment to a child before. How ironic that it would be Harold Park's daughter who pulled at Kit's heart strings with such force. Maybe it was because of Park's criminal background that Kit wanted the very best for that golden-haired little girl and her beautiful mother.

When Kit's father had been killed, he'd thought he'd experienced the very worst thing that could happen to a person. Though his father's killer had been killed, too, Kit hadn't been able to get over the pain. It took years of maturing to teach him that sometimes horrible things happened to the most innocent people. Other people suffered heartache, too. Ridding the world of the people who'd terrorized Natalie with frightening phone calls and break-ins had now become his first priority.

ON FRIDAY AT noon Kit walked into the interrogation room at the Leavenworth prison carrying an envelope. A prison guard stood by the door.

Esger was sitting behind a table with his ankles shackled. The balding man was sixty but looked older. His dark blue eyes studied Kit's star-shaped badge.

"You're excellent at what you do, Esger, I have to admit. Your forgeries fooled the very best for years. The inmates at Atwater sing your praises."

"Of course, but a Texas Ranger didn't come here to compliment me."

Kit took his time. "You're aging in here, Barni. I'm prepared to slice two years off your twelve-year sentence if you'll help me out on a particular case."

The prisoner stared at Kit for a long time. "What do you want to know?"

"Eight years ago Jimmy Salter and Harold Park made contact with you. I've got it on record that they came armed with a small fortune for you to transform their lives. " *Unfortunately those testimonials came from the inmates who knew Salter and were nothing more than hearsay.* "Now I'm here to find out if you made documents for their friends Juanita and Alonzo Morales, the husband and wife team working with them."

"They were brother and sister," Esger muttered before looking away. Kit was elated by that vital slip of information.

"That's it, Barni. That's all I want to know."

The forger cocked his head to the side. "So all I have to do is tell you that information and my sentence will be reduced by two years?"

"That's the deal. Your confession will be signed and notarized by the warden."

"How do you know I won't lie to you?"

"I don't. But if I find out later that you *did* lie—and I *will* find out—then I'll have your sentence extended for ten more years on the grounds of perjury before a federal officer of the United States.

"You've already served three years of your sentence. Doesn't it sound good to know two more years can be lopped off simply by telling the truth? You'd only have to serve seven more and be out of here by the time you're sixty-seven. There'd still be a lot of life to live, pictures to take of the Colorado mountains. Interested?"

Kit pulled a document out of the envelope and set

it in front of the prisoner along with a pen. "Go ahead and read it. Nothing will happen to you if you don't sign it. I'll walk out of here and you'll go on serving your original sentence."

Esger picked up the piece of paper and began to read. "This says I supplied documents to all four of them."

"That's right. If it's not true, then I'm wasting your time and mine."

His eyes narrowed on Kit. "Before I do anything, I want to talk to my attorney."

Kit nodded to the guard who opened the door. Esger's attorney entered the room, accompanied by a second guard. Kit stepped out to chat with the warden. After a few minutes Kit and the warden were allowed back inside.

"Well, Esger?" the warden asked.

The forger looked skeptical. "If I sign this, is it true I'll be out of here in seven years?"

"It is. But if you lie, that paper also states that ten years will be added to your original sentence. To make it legal and binding, I'll sign my name below yours. Your attorney will sign it and the guards will witness it. Won't it feel good to do something helpful for a change?"

Esger hesitated a moment longer and then signed the document. His attorney, the warden and the two witnesses followed suit.

Barni Esger's signature helped tie the loose ends together, making a solid case against three killers wanted by the FBI, one of whom was already dead. Kit had yet to learn what crimes Juanita had committed since her release from jail. But for now he couldn't have been happier.

He went to the warden's office and had a copy made of the signed confession before he left the prison with it and headed to the airport twenty-five miles away in Kansas City. He would have to hurry; his US Airways flight would be leaving at 4:00 p.m. That would put him in Austin around seven-thirty.

It was close to eight when he phoned TJ from his car in the airport parking lot to tell him the outcome of his visit to Leavenworth. "They're all involved in the LifeSpan embezzlement scheme. I'm waiting for a few more bits of information and then we can begin a manhunt for the Morales duo."

"That's fine work despite your unorthodox methods. Using the prison warden—that's a new one. I see you've logged a lot of flying miles in less than a week. Take a day off before you burn out. That's an order."

"In that case, I have a rodeo event I'd like to attend this Saturday and I'll need an officer to stay at the Harris home while I'm gone."

"I'll arrange it. Don't get stomped on."

"No, sir." With a laugh Kit hung up and started changing into his clerical shirt when his phone rang. He looked at the screen and took the call.

"Hey, Brandon—"

"Boy, am I glad you answered. I need your help in the worst way, bro."

"You mean you haven't found a hazer yet?"

"Yeah, I have. Corky Tibbs."

"I remember Corky. He's a great choice."

"I know. He said he'd haze for me until Scott is back, but he can't start for two weeks. I still haven't found anyone to ride for me in San Antonio tomorrow night."

Kit sucked in his breath. He'd thought he'd try to get there to watch his brother tomorrow night, but not to be part of the show. He'd turned him down once. Maybe he could help him out tomorrow night. But it all depended on Natalie, because he wasn't going to leave her unattended with Alonzo and Juanita still on the loose.

"Tell you what. Give me an hour and I'll phone you back if I can do it. That's the best I can offer."

"I knew I could count on you."

"Brandon—I only said if, so don't—"

His brother clicked off before Kit could finish the sentence.

After he hung up he finished putting on the shirt and took off for Natalie's house. En route he phoned Luckey. Kit had no idea if his friend would be available. He could be deep into a case or he might already have plans. But it was worth a try to find out.

"Well, if it isn't Father Segal," Luckey teased when the call connected.

Kit chuckled. "Tonight it's just plain Kit, even if I'm wearing a collar. I'm glad I could reach a live voice."

"Don't tell me you don't have anything to do on a Friday night because none of the guys would believe you. What's up?"

"My brother needs me to haze for him tomorrow night in San Antonio. Are you working a case or could you guard Natalie for me?"

"You mean at her house?"

"No. She says she likes the rodeo so I thought I'd take her and Amy with me so she can watch. I'd need your services during the event. Here's why."

He spent the next few minutes filling his friend in on the case. "One or both of the Moraleses is after the money and the guns. None of those items are in the house, and I'm convinced they'll come after Natalie when they break in again and realize that fact. She's not safe until they're caught."

"Sure I'll help. It'll be fun to watch you in the saddle."

"You don't have to do this, Luckey."

"You've helped me out plenty of times and my weekend is wide open. The boss told me to expect a new case on Monday."

"I'll owe you big time. I'm on my way home now. If Natalie says she wants to go with me, I'll call you and we'll make plans."

"Home, huh?"

"Don't start, Luckey."

"Yup. You have it bad. I'll wait for your call."

NATALIE HAD JUST put Amy down for the night when her cell rang. Her pulse raced before she answered. "Hi, Kit. Are you still in Kansas?"

"Nope. I'm pulling into the driveway and I wanted to give you a heads-up."

She was so happy he was back she had to be careful not to show it. "It's perfect timing. Amy's just fallen asleep. If she'd seen you, she wouldn't have wanted to go to bed. She said your name several times today. She can't figure out where you are." His chuckle worked its way to her insides.

She could hear the garage door opening while they were still on the phone. "Maybe we can fix that problem this weekend," he said and then disconnected, leaving her hanging.

When he walked into the kitchen wearing his collared shirt, her heart was still thudding. He looked... sensational. "Welcome back, Father Saunders. Would you care for something cold to drink?"

His gaze held hers. "I'd like a cola if you have one."

"I have a six-pack."

"Give me a minute to freshen up."

While he disappeared, she pulled two out of the fridge and went into the living room to wait for him. He returned quickly, wearing a polo shirt, and reached for his soda before he sat on the couch. After taking a long swallow he said, "How was your day?"

"Uneventful, thank heaven. How was yours?"

"My trip to Leavenworth turned all of my hunches into truths."

She sat forward in her chair. "Tell me everything."

"I made a deal with Esger, who signed a confession in front of the prison warden. In exchange, two years have been taken off his twelve-year prison sentence. He provided false ID to your husband, to Salter, to the other prisoner who escaped with your husband, Alonzo Morales, and to his sister, Juanita Morales.

"She probably drove the vehicle that took them to Fort Collins where they would have paid a fortune to Esger to fix them up with false documents. When they'd planned out their con, they came to Texas. The woman Colette saw with your husband was Juanita. I sent Colette a rap sheet on the other woman and she made a positive identification of the mug shot."

Natalie jumped to her feet. "Then two killers are still at large."

"That's true, but we know who they are and what they look like. Thanks to Colette, I'll be able to close in on them much sooner. When I've pieced a little more information together, I'll organize a manhunt to bring them in."

She stood there looking at him in awe. "You only took on this case a week ago, and already you know everything. You must have come to this earth with special gifts."

He darted her a quick smile. "No. I was born naturally curious. I was always asking why. It drove my family crazy."

"Be serious for a minute. Do you ever take a break?"

"I'm taking one this weekend."

Natalie didn't know what that meant. "I'm glad to hear you have a personal life. You must be sick of sleeping on the floor with one eye open all the time."

"I don't mind. It's all part of the job." He finished his cola. "How would you and Amy like to drive to San Antonio with me tomorrow? She's a great little traveler. We'll stay at a motel close to the arena and order a crib for your room. There's an animal exhibit at Little Buckaroo Farms Amy will love. You can push her around in her stroller."

What?

"I'm going to haze for my brother at the rodeo tomorrow night. My friend Luckey will guard you during the steer wrestling event. But if you don't want to come, a surveillance team will watch you here all weekend. The decision is yours."

Don't want to come? Natalie had trouble catching her breath. "I'd love to go, but I don't want you to feel you have to take us along. Amy and I will be fine here."

"Wouldn't you like a break that doesn't include traveling on a jet?"

"Well, yes, but—"

"But what?" he broke in, sounding tense all of a sudden.

"But nothing," she said with a smile he reciprocated, thrilling her out of her mind. Natalie sensed he wanted her with him and she wanted to be there. She was overjoyed that he'd invited her. "What time do you want to leave tomorrow?"

"Whenever we feel like it. The drive to San Antonio only takes an hour and a half. I'll need to meet Brandon at the arena an hour before his event. Why don't we take off after breakfast and check in at the motel before we visit the animals?"

"That sounds perfect. Amy will be worn out after that and take a nap before we go to the arena to watch you compete."

"Then it's settled. Now, if you'll excuse me, I have half a dozen phone calls to make."

She could imagine. "While you do that, I'll do a

little packing and get ready for tomorrow. See you in the morning."

For once she didn't mind saying good-night because she knew she'd be with Kit all weekend. She couldn't wait to watch him in the arena. Any time spent with him was precious.

By the time Natalie slid under the covers she knew she was suffering from a full-blown case of hero worship.

Truth really was stranger than fiction because in one week she'd fallen hard for the gorgeous Ranger. With every passing minute she was getting in deeper and deeper. Last night when he'd put his arms around her to comfort her, she'd struggled not to return the kiss he'd given her on the cheek. If only he knew how badly she'd ached for the taste and feel of his mouth on hers.

Chapter Six

"Look, Amy! That's a cow! A *big* one."

Kit chuckled as Amy imitated him and said, "Big cow." He'd been pushing her around in the stroller with Natalie at his side. Despite the heat, the Little Buckaroo Farm turned out to be pure delight. Seeing it through Amy's eyes made the experience so much fun, Kit didn't want it to end.

Hundreds of other families exclaimed over the animals. The goat-milking entertained everyone. "Shall we go see the horses now?" He pushed on and stopped in front of the fence so Amy could have a clear view of the horses in the corral.

Natalie leaned down. "See the horses?"

"Hus!" Amy pronounced. Both Kit and Natalie broke into laughter.

"That's right, little cutie," Kit agreed. "You're looking at a *big* hus."

When they least expected it, the bay closest to them let out a loud, high-pitched neigh that startled a lot of people and frightened Amy. "Kit!" She cried his name and squirmed around, holding up her arms. He undid the strap that held her and pulled her into his arms. She clung to him, crying her heart out.

A lot of bystanders smiled to see her hugging the priest. Natalie eyed the two of them. "If you had any question of how much she likes you, it's just been answered. You've received my daughter's seal of approval. She didn't even think to turn to me."

To hold her warm little body against him with her arms around his neck brought a huge lump to his throat. "I'm a grown man who was raised around horses and it startled me, too. I'm glad she feels safe with me. But maybe coming to the farm wasn't a good idea."

"Don't be silly. She loved it. She'll get over the scare."

When he would have put Amy back in the stroller, she fought to stay in his arms.

Natalie shot him a glance. "I think it's time to go back to the motel." He agreed.

She started pushing the stroller toward the main gate. He followed, carrying the precious princess who continued to let out shuddering little half sobs. By the time they'd reached Kit's car she'd calmed down.

He put Amy in her car seat, but she didn't like it. "I'll sit next to her," Natalie told him. "A nap is exactly what she needs."

After Kit put the stroller in the trunk of the Altima, he started the car and drove them to the Bucking Horse Motel near the arena. They had rooms side by side. He opened the rear door to help Natalie out.

"I think I'd better take her into my room without you, Kit. Otherwise she might never settle down."

"You're probably right, but let me make sure it's safe." After he'd checked the room, he came back out. "I'll call you when I'm ready to leave."

Once she'd lifted Amy into her arms, he handed her the diaper bag and watched as they disappeared inside. He got Amy's stroller out of the trunk and put it outside Natalie's room for Luckey to put in his car. He could hear Amy's whimpers as he let himself into his room.

His friend would already be inside. They'd arranged for him to arrive at the motel ahead of time so no one would be aware. His presence would free Kit to leave for the arena to meet Brandon, who'd arrive in his own truck and trailer. He'd be bringing Kit's favorite horse and his gear.

When he walked in, he saw his dark-blond friend stretched out on the bed in his Western clothes, watching TV.

"Thanks for coming. I appreciate you doing this big favor for me."

"Hey. This is the kind of work I like. Where's Mrs. Harris?"

"Next door. Room 14." He told Luckey what had happened at the farm. "Let's hope Amy has forgotten when she wakes up. The stroller is outside her door. Amy will be easier to handle if Natalie can wheel her around at the arena. Brandon has reserved seats for you on the front row near the chute."

"I've already got that covered."

"What do you mean?"

"Vic's here, too."

"What have you done?"

"I told the guys you were going to be the hazer tonight. Cy wanted to come, but he's on a case and can't leave. Vic was free and wants to watch you ride. He also wants to get a look at Natalie Harris. So do I."

Kit shook his head then laughed. In truth he was relieved two of the best Rangers alive would be helping to guard Natalie. "I have something to show you."

Luckey sat up. Kit pulled out a file and handed him the rap sheets with the mug shots on the Morales siblings. "I have to assume they've been watching the house, so it's possible that one of them might have followed us here and the other is planning to get into Natalie's house. One of the surveillance team will be inside, ready to arrest him or her on sight."

"Let's hope it happens, and then you can zero in on the killer still at large."

"I have no idea which one will be tailing Natalie and me. If it's Juanita, she could be in her old disguise of blond hair and blue eyes. But my hunch is on Alonzo who might even try to kidnap Amy or Natalie or both. I'd imagine they must be desperate to find the money and the guns."

Luckey put the rap sheets on the dresser. "Get your mind off the case and concentrate on helping your brother bring in the best time tonight. Leave the worry to Vic and me."

"I will." Kit clapped his friend on the shoulder and phoned Natalie. She picked up on the first ring.

"Kit?"

"How's Amy?"

"Blissfully asleep."

"Good."

"Are you ready to go?"

"Yup. I'm walking out the door. Luckey's here and he'll phone you when it's time to leave for the arena."

"I'm excited to watch you and your brother compete."

"I haven't hazed for him in a while."

"Don't give me that bull. No pun intended." He laughed. "I happen to know a hazer has to foresee all possibilities of trouble and correct them in a split second. You couldn't turn in a bad performance if you tried."

"I'm flattered by your confidence in me. See you back here after the rodeo. Stay safe."

"You, too. Go get 'em, cowboy!"

Luckey stared at him as he hung up. "Yup," he murmured.

"Don't say it. Don't say anything."

"Oh, I won't!" A big grin broke out on his tanned face. "That conversation said it all."

"See you later. I'm out of here."

Kit left the room still wearing his clerical shirt and got into his car. He'd stowed his riding clothes and cowboy hat in the trunk. Brandon would be waiting for him in his trailer behind the livestock pens.

He checked his rearview mirror repeatedly on the way to see if anyone was following him, but he saw nothing suspicious.

Kit arrived to find his brother standing outside with one of his team members. The second he saw him, Brandon ran to the car, practically pulling Kit out of the driver's seat to give him a hug. "Thanks, bro. You're saving my life. I know you're on a case."

"It's all right. I've got it covered."

His brother did a double-take when he pulled away from him. "What are you doing in that outfit?"

"Part of my cover. Let's go inside the trailer so I can change."

"Where's your gear?"

"In the trunk."

"I'll get it." Brandon was so grateful, it was as if he couldn't do enough for his older brother. It didn't take long for Kit to put on his rodeo clothes.

"Terry's already walked our horses inside," Brandon informed him.

"How's Flash?"

"The vet checked both horses over this morning. Yours is in great condition. I've seen to that. Let's go."

The familiar smell of the animals took Kit back to the time when he'd competed on a regular basis. It seemed a lifetime ago. Since then so much in his life had changed, starting with his move to Austin and the beginning of his career as a Ranger. He'd gained three close friends who were like brothers.

He loved this life.

If he hadn't chosen this profession, he would never have met Natalie. The thought of any harm coming to her or Amy filled him with rage. But he needed to take Luckey's advice and stay centered on the job ahead of him for Brandon's sake.

If his brother could win the national championship in Las Vegas, the prize money would be enough to keep the family ranch running. Kit determined to do his best for him.

Flash, Kit's black-and-white gelding, nickered as Kit rubbed his forelock. "Good to see you, buddy. I've missed you, too." He slipped his horse some sugar cubes. "I'm going to eat my pre-competition Snickers, so you should be able to binge, too."

He saddled and bridled Flash. After putting on his riding gloves, he joined his brother in the corral to put his horse through some paces. With the right animal, everything felt right. Flash felt right beneath him.

Brandon rode alongside him. "It's like old times, bro."

Kit nodded. "Feels good to be riding with you again."

"You don't know what it means to me."

"Sure I do."

"Scott feels terrible."

"I can imagine, but accidents happen. Corky will do a great job for you."

Brandon checked his watch. "It's time for me to head back in for the parade."

"I'll be right beside you when it's time. I bet you'll do it under 3 seconds." To bring down the steer in 2.9 would be hard to do but it wasn't impossible.

"I've got to get in that range to keep my average."

"Hold that thought." They high-fived.

Kit watched with pride as his brother rode in. Flash was frisky so he rode him around for a while then headed to the arena to wait their turn. Natalie would be in the bleachers by now.

He patted his horse. "We've got to do our best tonight. Brandon needs a win and we don't want to disappoint Natalie with a poor performance."

In the background he could hear the "Star Spangled Banner" sung by a local country singer, then the roar of the crowd and the applause. Finally came the announcements to open the San Antonio Rodeo.

"This is it." He walked Flash inside to a place where the other hazers were lined up. Some of the riders were familiar and they nodded to him. Because of his standings, Brandon would be second out of the box. Kit found his spot in line. Before long it was time for him to back into the box on the timed-event side of the arena.

"Next up, Brandon Saunders, mounted on his champion horse Ringo, from Marble Falls, Texas. Tonight his substitute hazer is Miles Saunders. They were known in the past as the dynamic brother duo!"

Kit heard a roar from the crowd. He watched his brother on the other side of the chute. He looked fierce. Kit knew that rush of adrenaline every rider experienced while they waited. When Brandon nodded his head, they released the steer and Kit rocketed out of the box to bookend the steer and ride close enough to touch it. Brandon picked it off fast while Kit rode on to rein in his brother's horse.

"That's a time of 3.0! Brandon is definitely on his game tonight!"

A huge roar went up from the crowd again.

The relief Kit felt left him overjoyed for his brother. After losing Scott, he'd had to fight through the bitter disappointment, but tonight he'd pulled it off. When the last steer wrestler had performed, the announcer said Brandon's time was the best of the night. *Hallelujah*.

Since his brother had to wait around to pick up his gold buckle for the night, Kit left both horses with Brandon's team and walked back to the trailer to get his clothes and put them in his car. Then he headed to the bleachers. Now that his part was over, the only thing driving him was the need to be with Natalie.

Even from a distance he spotted her gleaming honey-blond hair. He had no idea where Luckey or Vic had positioned themselves, but it didn't matter because she looked happy. There was an empty seat next to her and Amy sat in her stroller in front of her, drinking water from a bottle.

As he walked toward her he heard a familiar voice. "Miles?"

It was his mother, but he'd been so intent on reaching Natalie, he was slow on the uptake. She sat on Natalie's right side and grasped his hand. "I'm so proud of you boys I could burst."

"Thanks, Mom."

He bent to kiss her cheek, but his gaze had centered on another pair of eyes that were focused on him, glowing a hot green. Kit moved past his mother.

"You were fantastic out there," Natalie said in a quiet voice. "Come and sit down."

As he stepped around the stroller and took his seat, Amy saw him and held up her hands, dropping the water bottle. "Kit!"

Not immune to that entreaty, he undid the strap and pulled Amy into his arms. "Did you see the horses?"

"Hus." She gave him a big smile and kissed his cheek several times. The gesture went straight to his heart, as did Natalie's smile. The bareback riding event had gotten under way, but Kit couldn't concentrate on anything while he held Natalie's daughter on his lap.

"You have a new little rodeo fan, Father Segal. And here you were, hoping you could still pull it off. If you want my opinion, they should give you hazers a gold buckle. Your mother agrees with me."

"How much does she know about us?" he whispered.

"Your brother told her I'm a friend," she whispered back. "I've enjoyed sitting next to her. She taught me a lot about steer wrestling while we watched."

Kit should have remembered his mother would be here to cheer them on. It hadn't occurred to him that the two would meet.

Luckey and Vic had to be around here somewhere. The rodeo would go on for another half hour, but for his friends' sake Kit didn't want to force them to be here any longer. Besides, Amy was restless. "Get ready to leave when the bareback riding ends. I'll carry the stroller while you bring Amy."

"Okay."

He moved Amy into her arms. The diaper bag sat behind the seat of the stroller. He picked up the water bottle and stowed it inside. As soon as the announcer called for the tie-roping to start, Kit stood and carried the stroller past several fans to the aisle on the other

side of him. Natalie followed with Amy who hadn't
liked being moved. He'd talk to his mother later.

When they reached the parking area he headed
straight for his car and put the stroller in the trunk.
Once he'd unlocked the car, Natalie fastened Amy in
the car seat. He held the front door open for her and
then went around to slide in behind the steering wheel.

Relief swept through him that his brother had the
winning time. But more than that, he was thankful
there'd been no incident to mar the night for them. He
watched to see if they were being followed. En route
to the motel his cell rang. He attached his Bluetooth
earpiece and answered.

"Great job out there!"

"Thanks, Luckey. I take it you didn't spot Morales
or his sister."

"Not tonight."

"I'm relieved to hear it. You're free to go and enjoy
the rest of your evening."

"I'll tell Vic."

"Good. Just remember I'm here for you guys when
you need my help."

"We know that. It was a real pleasure meeting Mrs.
Harris. I told Vic I wish I'd met her first. She's a stun-
ner, and even better, she's nice."

"Agreed." Nice went a long way in Kit's book, too.
"Talk to you later." He ended the call.

Kit flashed Natalie a sideways glance, loving the
sight of her profile. She was feminine to the core. "If
there was no threat, we could have stayed through the

whole program. Sorry to have to pull you away if you were enjoying it."

"It was the perfect time to leave. Amy kept squirming. I was pretty sure I'd have to take her out when she'd finished her water." She turned toward him. "Your mother is a lovely person. I can see where you get your coloring."

"Most people think I look like my dad."

"Then he must have been one tall and attractive Texas Ranger, too."

"Luckey's the one the females flock to," Kit said to hide his emotions. "He's still single—that's why we nicknamed him Luckey."

She chuckled. "What about Ranger Malone? Is Vic his real name?"

"He's part Lipan Apache. His Ranger ancestor was named Victorio and Vic was named for him. But he likes the short version."

"That's fascinating. And how did you get the name Kit?"

"When I first joined the Rangers, my boss said, 'Your reputation at the police academy precedes you. Like Kit Carson, "You're clean as a hound's tooth."' The nickname stuck."

"I can't imagine a greater compliment. It fits you to a tee. I can vouch for that myself. If your father were alive, he would have been proud of you and your brother tonight."

"I'm sure you're right."

"Your mom was ecstatic."

"You know mothers."

"Yes. I had a great one, too."

"It shows."

"Thank you," she whispered.

"Have you noticed Amy's fallen asleep?"

"She's had a big day."

"And a big scare from a big hus."

Natalie's quiet laughter stayed with him. Before long they arrived at the motel and he drove to the parking space in front of his room. Kit wanted to stay in the moment and not get out. The need to take her into his arms was so strong he turned to reach for her, but there was a knock on the window.

He jerked around in surprise, thinking it must be one of the guys.

Janie?

In the next breath he opened the door and got out of the car.

"Sorry, Kit. I didn't mean to startle you."

Kit couldn't concentrate because Natalie had gotten out of the car and had opened the back door to retrieve Amy.

"I promised Scott I'd come to watch Brandon's performance and take pictures. Your brother said you were staying at the Bucking Horse. Scott wanted me to thank you for pinch-hitting for him. It's because of you that Brandon wound up with a 3.0."

He looked back at Janie, barely registering her comments. "Tell Scott I'm sorry about his accident. We're all hoping he gets better soon so he can end the season in Las Vegas with Brandon." He closed the door and locked the car with the remote.

"I will. It's…it's wonderful to see you again, Kit."

"It's good to see you, too. Now, if you'll excuse me, I have to go in." He started to leave. She followed him.

"Brandon didn't tell me you're seeing someone. I was so surprised when I saw her sitting by your mom."

A lifetime ago he might have been glad that she minded, but not anymore. If anything, he was irritated that she hadn't called him on the phone to tell him all this. Or better yet, hadn't made contact at all. If he were Scott, he wouldn't be happy to know his wife was here alone talking to her old boyfriend. Her unexpected appearance had shattered the moment for Kit.

"Be safe driving home," was all he said before he headed for Natalie's door.

Once inside the motel room, Natalie had put a sleeping Amy in the crib then darted over to the window to look through the curtain. The attractive dark-blonde woman talking to Kit obviously knew him well. Natalie felt a stab of jealousy she couldn't help.

For the woman to come up to the car to get his attention spoke of long-time familiarity. Kit's jaw had hardened when he'd recognized her. Until she'd knocked on the window, Natalie had felt Kit might have been going to kiss her. But in an instant the mood had been broken.

She jumped when she heard the soft knock on the door. Natalie smoothed the hair off her hot cheeks and opened it. "Hi."

"Is Amy still asleep?"

"Yes."

"We need to talk." He spoke in a quiet tone and

walked in, locking the door behind him. "I shouldn't have let you come into the room alone before I could check it."

"I wasn't thinking."

"For once I wasn't concentrating. It was a slip that could have ended in disaster. Sit down while I call the front desk and ask them to bring in a cot. I'll be sleeping by you tonight. I'll tell them to put it outside the door so it won't wake Amy."

She was so happy he was going to stay with her, she could hardly contain it. He walked over to the bedside table and phoned housekeeping. Then he sat on the side of the bed while she sank into a chair.

"I take it that woman is a friend of yours."

His gaze traveled over her features. "She's Scott's wife. They have a little boy."

"Oh!" That was enough to stifle her fear that he was in an ongoing relationship with her.

"I knew her long before any of us knew Scott."

Her heart plummeted. "Us?"

"Brandon and me. Janie was my girlfriend during our steer wrestling days. I thought the day would come when we would get married."

"What happened?"

"I decided to go into law enforcement rather than be a rancher. She knew the pain our family had gone through when our father died. To know I'd chosen a career that had killed my father upset her to the point that she broke up with me."

Groan. "That must have been devastating."

"I suffered for a while. But time passed and I realized it was the best thing that could have happened. She met Scott—a good, steady rancher and horseman. I was free to do the work I enjoy, knowing I wasn't tearing my wife apart because she was afraid for me." He sat forward. "Luckey had a wife like that. After a year they divorced because she couldn't take it."

"I can understand that. Are you over Janie?"

"A long time ago," he said without hesitation.

That sounded definite. After a pause she added, "Do you think she's over you?"

"Yes. I'm convinced she tracked me down here because she was curious to see the woman who was sitting at the rodeo with my mother."

"I presume that was her coveted place for a long time. I get it. Did you tell her who I was?"

"I said nothing and told her I had to go in. I'm working on your case, but my brother got careless and told her where I was staying. He knows better, but he forgot. It's the reason I don't have much of a personal life while I'm on a case."

"It's all right, Kit."

"No, it isn't." He got to his feet and put his hands on his hips. His brows met in a frown. "I promised to protect you, but I let my brother's need take precedence over my duty to you. Never again."

"Your boss had it right. Like Kit Carson, you're as clean as a hound's tooth. Cut yourself some slack for getting interrupted by your old girlfriend. That wasn't your fault. Don't forget that two of your Ranger buddies guarded me at the rodeo. If anyone is to blame, it's me, for getting out of the car before you told me to. I'm the one who could have walked in on someone waiting in the room."

"Thank heaven it was empty," he muttered with emotion. "If Morales had been inside, he could have taken you and Amy hostage. If my boss knew what had happened, he'd probably throw me out of the Rangers and he would have every justification."

Natalie got up from the chair. "I see why you're so upset. This has taught me a lesson, too. I'll follow your directions to the letter. Will that be good enough for you?"

His rigid body relaxed and he let out a deep sigh. "It's going to have to be. Why don't you get ready for bed while I see if they've brought the cot?"

"Okay."

Natalie disappeared into the bathroom and got undressed. Her pajamas and robe were hanging on the hook on the back of the door. She put everything on and brushed her teeth. When she came out, she noticed the cot opened up in front of the TV. Kit had pushed a chair into the corner and was talking on his cell phone.

She took a peek at Amy then got into the double bed, turning on her side away from him.

A few minutes later the light went out. She heard the creaking of the cot. Kit had to be exhausted. "Kit?"

"Yes?"

"My heart was in my throat when your event was announced. The second the chute opened, it looked like two torpedoes shot forward. It was over so fast I didn't have time to blink. What both of you did out there today was incredible. You have to be thrilled. You know your brother is thankful. So enjoy the triumph of this night. Please."

Maybe five minutes passed before he spoke, but it wasn't the comment she'd expected. "That's hard to do. Vic got into trouble on a case because of a mistake he made. It almost cost him his badge."

"What happened?"

"Someone kidnapped his son from elementary school."

"Oh, no—"

"The guy was caught and arrested. When Vic interrogated him at the jail, the kidnapper refused to tell him where he'd taken his son. Vic went crazy and grabbed him. I saw him through the window and stepped in to stop him."

"He was only trying to find his son."

"True. But he forgot to be careful. That's what happened to me tonight. It won't happen again."

"Did he find his son?"

"Yes, thank God."

Kit wasn't about to let this go and she realized there was nothing she could say that would make him feel better. Naturally he'd been distracted by the woman he'd once planned to marry. But Natalie reasoned to herself that if he had loved her more than anything, he wouldn't have become a Ranger.

When she'd given up hope of any more talk he spoke again. "The only way I can savor this night is knowing you and Amy weren't harmed because of my distraction. You have to know your little girl is adorable. I'll never forget the look of fright on her face when that horse neighed. She hugged me so hard, I can still feel it."

"Her response was instinctive." Natalie had witnessed it. Anyone watching would have thought Kit was her father. Amy knew where to turn for safety and affection. Not in all the time Rod had lived at the house did he embrace Amy like that.

"Get a good sleep, Natalie."

"I could wish the same for you, but I know that as long as you're guarding me, you'll never get the kind of sleep you need."

"I manage."

Tears trickled out of her eyes onto the pillow. *Sweet, wonderful Kit...*

AFTER PHONING THE officer inside the house to let him know they were back, Kit drove the Altima into Natalie's garage at six Sunday evening. Much as he would have loved for them to stay and play in the swimming pool at the motel and not come home until dark, he refused to take any more unnecessary risks while Morales and his sister were still at large. Instead they stopped at several parks to allow Amy to run around while he stood guard, then drove home and ate their meals en route.

Kit helped Natalie inside with Amy. While she took care of her daughter, he went into the den with the officer and shut the door.

"Now we can talk. Tell me what's gone on."

"No one tried to break in, but several people came to the house. The first person rang the bell about one yesterday afternoon. The man left a lawn care brochure on the front door handle. I put it on the kitchen table. Today a couple of women knocked on the door around eleven. They were Jehovah Witnesses and left the *Watchtower* magazine."

"While you're still here, I'll pull the tape on the camera." Kit walked through the house to the front door and opened it. After he returned to the study they looked at the footage. "The lawn man doesn't resemble Morales, but could have been paid by him to case the place."

Kit kept looking until he saw the women. "They're the wrong ages and body shapes to impersonate Juanita. But they could be working for her."

"Maybe they've decided the money and guns aren't here and the people who came by the house were on the level."

"Maybe," Kit muttered. "Thanks for doing a great job. I'll take over from here."

He walked the officer to the back door. When he'd gone, Kit gathered the material left on the kitchen table and went to the den. First he called the Better Business Bureau and learned that Greenside Lawn Service was a legitimate business. Next he contacted the company to verify the employment of the man whose name had been stamped on the pamphlet. Everything checked out.

After phoning the Jehovah Witnesses Kingdom Hall number printed on the magazine, Kit asked if their people had been passing out magazines in northwest

Austin. No one could give him a definitive answer. Call back tomorrow.

He intended to do that after he went to the office in the morning. Kit had already set up a 9:00 a.m. meeting with the FBI agent working on the accounting investigation at LifeSpan. While he was checking some new emails on his laptop, his phone rang. He picked up when he saw who was calling.

"Cy? I thought you were on a case."

"I am, and something has turned up that might have a bearing on yours. Can you talk?"

"Yes."

"When I gave TJ an update on my investigation, he informed me about your case and suggested we share any new information."

"Does he see a link?"

"I think it's more of a hunch."

"If you're coming in to headquarters in the morning, let's talk then. I plan to be there by six-thirty."

"I'll be in around seven and find you."

"Sounds good."

"Luckey told me you nailed it at the rodeo. That's no surprise. Brandon could very well be the champion in December."

"We're hoping."

"So how are the widow and the priest? I've felt left out."

Kit's smile turned into a chuckle. "You guys never give up."

"As I recall you were relentless while I was protecting Kellie. Has the boss's advice been a help?"

He took a deep breath. "You *know* it hasn't."

"Yup. That's what I thought. See you in the morning." He was gone before Kit had a chance to say goodbye.

Kit would need surveillance on Natalie first thing in the morning. He made one more call, this time to headquarters to set it up. No sooner had he rung off than his phone sounded again. It was ten after ten. His mother. He'd been expecting this.

"Hi, Mom."

"I hope you have a minute to talk. We didn't get a chance at the arena. Thank you for hazing for Brandon. Thank you for being a wonderful son." Kit heard the tears in her voice.

"Luckily the captain gave me a day off that allowed me to do it."

"Brandon was so grateful. He told me Mrs. Harris is a friend of yours."

He'd been waiting for her to say something about Natalie. "She is."

"That little girl of hers is darling."

"Agreed. Mom? I'm still working on a case so I'll have to say good-night."

"All right."

"When this latest one is wrapped up, we'll all get together and take a little trip somewhere." He knew his mother worried about her bachelor sons, but that was an area where he couldn't help her out.

"I'd love that!"

"So would I, but I've got to go. Love you, Mom. Talk to you soon."

By the time he walked through the house to check the locks and turn off the lights, he discovered Natalie had gone to bed. Their talk last night had changed the atmosphere between them. She'd blamed herself for getting out of the car before he'd given her the signal.

All day she'd been careful to do everything right. Now she'd disappeared on him. He needed this case to be solved so they could behave naturally with each other.

Janie's unexpected appearance had made him realize he'd crossed the line in his mind. And in so doing, he'd left himself vulnerable. That meant he'd have to watch every step to ensure Natalie and Amy's safety, but it was getting harder and harder to do. Against his better judgment, his desire for Natalie had been growing, and now all he really wanted to do was to pull her into his arms and kiss her senseless.

Chapter Seven

Kit's watch alarm went off at six. He got up and out of the house before anyone else stirred. After leaving a note on the counter that he'd be at headquarters if Natalie needed to talk to him, he left in his car. A rug-cleaning service van was parked across the street. He nodded to the guys and drove downtown.

At work he stopped in the makeshift lunch room where he poured two cups of coffee and grabbed a couple of doughnuts. When he reached his office, the first thing he saw was a forensics report in his in-basket. He put the food on the desk and reached for the printout.

The DNA from the black hair found in Rodney Harris's car was a match for the DNA of felon Juanita Morales. Kit didn't need to read the rest. The case was coming together. Where in the hell were she and Alonzo hiding out? How soon could Natalie expect another visit?

"Kit?"

Cy had arrived. "Come on in and have breakfast with me."

"Don't mind if I do." They sat across from each

other. Cy bit into a doughnut. "The guys were right. Anyone would think you're a priest." He squinted at his friend. "Is the collar providing enough protection?"

"What do you think?" Kit muttered before taking a sip of the hot coffee.

"I can only speak from my own experience. A week into my undercover role as Kellie's husband and I wanted it to be real. I take it that's the place where you are about now."

"You're not a Ranger for nothing." Kit let out a frustrated sigh. "I swear I'm going to go crazy if I don't catch up with the Morales duo soon."

Cy leaned forward to reach for his cup. "That's why I'm here. After talking with TJ, I sent you an email. Open it and take a look."

Kit turned to the computer and found Cy's email.

Marcos Garcia, 63, of Sunset Valley, Austin, Texas, convicted of wire fraud affecting a financial institution, has been sentenced to 18 months in prison. He's been ordered to pay restitution totaling $400,000 by US District Court Judge Richard Salazar.

The Assistant US Attorney who handled the case stated that Garcia was an employee of the Empire Guaranty Mortgage Company based in Houston. He was responsible for preparing loan packages and forwarding the documents to financial institutions that provide financing and advisory services for assets management.

Kit looked up from his reading. "How do loan packages like these work?"

"In legal transactions, financial institutions purchase loans originated by mortgage companies, allowing the mortgage company to receive immediate payment and the financial institution to collect the interest."

"How exactly was Garcia implicated?"

"During this scheme, he signed a number of loan documents using various names. He forwarded these documents to multiple investor financial institutions, one of which was Austin Metroplex Bank. In effect, Garcia set it up so that there were numerous loans all connecting back to a single property, a fact that was not disclosed to the financial institutions."

"Ah."

"The proceeds of the fraudulent loans were subsequently wired into the account of a company associated with Empire Guaranty Mortgage Company. It's a bogus company. The name Julia Varoz comes up on the records, but there's no live body to prove she exists. As a result of Garcia's actions, Austin Metroplex Bank was one of nine financial institutions to suffer a loss. The total fraud scheme amounted to approximately twenty-five million dollars."

Kit let out a whistle. "Why does TJ feel this case touches on the one I'm investigating?"

Cy's brows lifted. "Julia Varoz is missing and so is four-hundred-thousand dollars. You're looking for Juanita and Alonzo Morales. One or both of them ransacked Natalie Harris's house looking for that exact sum of money."

"So TJ is thinking Julia could be Juanita, but the alias hasn't come up on the criminal index."

"Not yet. The connection I see is that Park withdrew four-hundred thousand from his account the day before he was murdered. Garcia owes that amount in restitution for his crime, but he's behind bars and Julia Varoz is missing."

"So maybe all four of them have been pulling off two cons at the same time," Kit mused aloud.

"It's possible."

Kit's thoughts shot ahead. "Juanita might be the girlfriend trying to find that money to help Garcia when he's released from prison. Maybe she turned on Harold."

"I don't know. But think about it… Garcia's only serving an eighteen-month sentence. Maybe Park double-crossed them and hid the money where they couldn't get at it."

"Esger made fraudulent documents for Juanita, but she might have found another forger to make her a new Varoz alias in order to run that dummy account for Garcia. But to find the right forger is a tough order."

"Yup." Cy finished off his coffee. "I've got to get going, but I wanted to give you something to chew on. Knowing you, you'll find the common denominator."

"Back at you. Your instincts are never wrong, Cy. Neither are TJ's. This could be huge."

He stood. "We'll just keep pecking away."

"Amen to that."

Deep in thought after Cy left, Kit went to the conference room to meet with the FBI agent working on the LifeSpan accounting fraud. He added his input. After they concluded their meeting, he left the building for the Kingdom Hall Center.

As soon as Natalie put Amy down for her nap at two, she went into the kitchen and called the nursing home in Denver. Today a service had been held for Amy's great-grandmother. The older woman had been on Natalie's mind.

"Cottonwood Nursing Home."

"Hello. My name is Natalie Harris. I'm calling to speak to someone who handled the funeral service for Gladys Park earlier today."

"Oh. That would be Mrs. Issac. I'll connect you." In a moment another voice came on the line.

"Hello? Mrs. Harris?"

"Yes. Thank you for answering. I want to know how the service went for Gladys Park. I sent flowers and wondered if you'd received them."

"We certainly did. The carnations were just lovely."

"I'm glad. Can you tell me anything about the service?"

"Well, the pastor said a few words and then one of the patients here spoke. Several of her friends from the church came. Also the podiatrist who took care of her sore feet right before she died. Gladys was well loved."

"I'm so glad to hear it. By any chance was there a picture taken? I'd like to have one for my daughter's scrapbook."

"I did take some for the pastor with his camera. He wanted to post the photos at the church in Gladys's memory and asked me to be sure I caught one of the floral arrangement with her name on it in gold letters."

"I'd love to have copies. Could I have his phone number?"

"Of course. You left your information when you were here. I'll email his number to you right now."

"Thank you so much."

"You're very welcome."

Natalie got off the phone and opened her laptop. As soon as she received the information, she phoned the number of Pastor Sidney Clark. Her call went to his voice mail. She left a message with her phone number and hung up.

She had no idea when she'd hear from him. Time was weighing heavy on her hands. Kit hadn't called and he'd left early this morning. Amy had asked for him several times throughout the day, and every time the little girl said his name, it echoed in Natalie's heart.

It was no good waiting for the phone to ring. She picked it up and dialed Jillian, but her voice mail picked up, as well. Colette would be at work, so it would be better to talk to her tonight.

Natalie went to her bedroom and turned on her TV. She skimmed through the channels. As she was trying to get interested in a program on supernovas, her cell rang. The screen indicated a Colorado area code. She reached for it and said hello.

"Mrs. Harris? This is Pastor Clark returning your call."

"Thank you so much, Pastor. I spoke with Mrs. Issac from the nursing home and I understand you had pictures taken at the service for Gladys Park."

"Yes. For the posting board in the foyer of the church. I like our flock to know and remember our church members."

"That's a lovely thing to do. She's my daughter's great-grandmother. I've made a baby book for her and I'd love to have copies of the photos. Would it be possible for you to send them to me?

"Of course. I'll ask my secretary to forward them to your email address." Natalie gave him her information; he promised to take care of it right away.

"You have no idea how much this means to me. Before we hang up, could you tell me how long you knew Gladys?"

"Oh, my, maybe twenty years. She and her husband Joseph were faithful members."

"I married her grandson late in her life and only met her last week. I took my daughter with me so she could see her."

"I visited her later that very day," he commented. "She told me how happy your visit made her. Bless you for coming to see her. She died holding on to that memory."

Natalie's eyes filled with tears. Without Kit, that trip to Denver would never have happened. "I'm thankful she had you to watch over her, Pastor. You don't know how much I appreciate your kindness. Do you know where she was interred?"

"Fairmount Cemetery next to her husband and their son and his wife."

"One day when my daughter is older, we'll go there. I'll look forward to receiving those photos. Thanks again."

"You're welcome, Mrs. Harris. God bless you."

Thrilled to have made contact, Natalie got off the phone and went to the kitchen to make some kind of a treat for Kit to thank him. She took her laptop with her and put it on the kitchen table.

What would he love? After some thought she decided to make brownies. Once they'd cooled she would ice them with peppermint frosting then pour melted chocolate chips over the top. The trick was to cut them into squares before the chocolate set. Her mom's recipe had always been a huge hit.

An hour later Amy awakened. Natalie brought her into the kitchen and set her up so she could play with the tins in the kitchen cupboard. She dangled the measuring spoons on a ring in front of her. Amy saw them. "Mama." She lifted her hands.

"Say 'spoons.'"

"Spoons."

"Yes." She kissed her cheeks. "Spoons."

Laughter bubbled out of Natalie. She found a wooden spoon so her daughter could pound on the bottoms of the saucepans. While she started cutting the brownies, she heard the text alert from her phone and glanced at the screen.

Driving into the garage.

Kit was home! Joy, joy, joy.

WHEN KIT WALKED into the house he was bombarded by the delicious smell of chocolate. He had to stop when he reached the kitchen because Amy sat surrounded by pots and pans and utensils, blocking his path.

"Kit!" She showed him the measuring spoons she held in one hand. "Spoons!" In the other she gripped a wooden spoon that she pounded on everything she could find. He burst into laughter and got down on his haunches. Picking up a potato masher, he tapped along on a couple of tins.

In the midst of all this he shot Natalie a glance. In her nautical-striped top and white shorts, those long legs made his breath catch. "I think your daughter might be turning into a drummer. Look at her go!"

Her radiant smile was unexpected after the tension between them last night. "I've been listening to her repertoire since she got up from her nap. Show her the ice cream scoop and ask her what it is."

He did as she suggested and held it in front of Amy. "What's this?"

"Scoop!"

Her answer amused him so much he picked up a heart-shaped cookie cutter. "What's this?"

"Cookie!"

That was close enough. He was having too much fun to quit. He found the spatula and lifted it.

"Spat!" She'd put her heart into it.

"Yes. *Spat*ula. You're even smarter than I realized." Kit leaned forward and kissed the top of her golden curls. She smelled sweet, like Natalie. Heavenly.

"You're home early," Natalie observed.

He looked up into those fabulous green eyes. "Yup. I could smell those brownies all the way to headquarters and decided to come home in time to sample them. Is that permitted?"

"I made them for you." She put half a dozen of the small squares on a plate and carried it to the table with some napkins.

"What's the occasion?"

He watched her open a jar of Vienna sausages and hand her daughter one. "It's a special thank-you. Would you like coffee or tea?"

"How about milk?"

"Coming right up." She poured him a glass and brought it to the table. Kit got up from the floor and joined her.

"What did I do to deserve all this?"

"I talked to the pastor who officiated at the service for Gladys today. He said our visit gave her peace before she died." Kit could tell she was fighting tears. "I'll never forget that you made that visit possible. You could have gone on your own to get information. But being the kind of person you are, you included Amy and me, even though it would have been easier for you to go alone."

"It was my pleasure, Natalie."

"You're such a good man. The pastor said that Gladys and Joseph Park were revered members of the congregation. That means everything to me. One day I'll take Amy to visit her grandparents and great-grandparents at the cemetery." She cleared her throat. "He had pictures taken at the service to post at his church. I asked him to email me copies for Amy's baby book."

"Have they come yet?"

"I'll look after I put Amy in the high chair. It's time for her dinner."

While she dealt with her daughter he started eating the brownies and couldn't stop until he'd eaten every one. "Are the rest of the brownies in the pan for me, too?"

She looked down at his empty plate with a faint smile. "What do *you* think?"

"I think you've won my allegiance for life. You could have a million-dollar career selling these."

"I'm glad you like them."

"I promise to save you one."

"Don't worry about it. I can always make another batch."

"Promise?"

Her eyes smiled at him before she fed her daughter some carrots and beef from the baby food jar. He got busy putting everything on the floor back in the drawers and cupboards. By now Amy was being treated to some Goldfish crackers. Her eyes lit up. "Fish!"

Kit grabbed one and put it in his mouth. "Fish. Yum!"

"Yum," she mimicked. He laughed.

Natalie grinned as she checked her emails. "Better watch what you say around her. She's a sponge."

Kit ate another fish and Amy promptly imitated him.

"Oh, good! The pictures have come. There are two

of them. One of the casket and the other a group photo."
She studied them for a minute. "The secretary took
the time to label each person. How nice. The flowers
on the casket are beautiful. Take a look." She slid the
laptop in front of Kit.

He knew these pictures meant a lot to Natalie, but
the people held no significance for him until he saw
the name Dr. Varoz.

She had blond hair, but it was *Juanita Morales*. He'd
bet his life on it.

By the merest chance he'd found the woman Cy
was searching for in relation to the mortgage fraud
case. There was no time to lose. He flicked his gaze
to Natalie.

"Excuse me for a second. I need to call the director
of the nursing home right away."

"Use my phone. I called Mrs. Issac not too long ago,
so her number should be right there in my call history."

"Thank you." He waited for his call to be answered
then asked to speak to the director.

"This is she."

"It's Father Segal calling from Austin."

"Oh, yes, Father. How can I help you?"

"Mrs. Reese just shared the photos from the service for Gladys Park. Can you tell me about the blond
woman, Dr. Varoz? She was in the group photo. Was
she a church member, too?"

"No. She filled in for the regular podiatrist who
went on vacation."

"Who was that?"

"Dr. Nyman."

"I see. How many times did Dr. Varoz come to see Gladys?"

"Just once, last Friday. Gladys was feeling poorly so she stayed awhile to keep her company."

"Do you know why she came to the service?"

"She'd been at the nursing home to see another patient. I guess she decided to attend the service since she'd spent time with Gladys on Friday."

It meant Gladys hadn't supplied her with the information she'd been looking for. Today she'd hung around; possibly hoping to find out where Gladys's possessions were located.

"Can you tell us who handled her financial arrangements? Mrs. Harris would like to get in touch with them."

"The attorney for Mrs. Park."

"Do you have a name?"

"Let me check. Yes, here it is. The firm of Farbes and Lowell." She gave him the phone number.

"Thank you for that information. Sorry to bother you."

"No problem at all."

He hung up and gave Natalie her phone. "I'll be right back."

On an adrenaline rush he hurried into the den and phoned Cy on his cell. "Come on, bud. Pick up."

The second he heard his friend's voice he pounced. "You'll never guess who was at the funeral service for Harold Park's grandmother today. Julia Varoz, alias Juanita Morales."

"What?"

"Yup. TJ's hunch paid off. I'm looking at a picture of her as we speak. She's wearing her blond disguise, posing as a podiatrist for Gladys Park. That puts her in Denver earlier today. When Natalie's house was ransacked and no money was found, she must have left for Denver. This is the break we've both been looking for."

"I'm calling TJ. We need to put out an APB on her immediately."

"I'll email you the picture from Natalie's laptop and meet you at headquarters."

He ended the call with Cy and phoned downtown to get the surveillance team back to guard Natalie. When he started for the kitchen he discovered she'd taken Amy into the living room to play with her toys.

She stared at him. "What did you see in those photos that sent you flying out of the room?"

"Juanita Morales."

Natalie gasped.

"She was the assumed podiatrist while the real doctor was on vacation. Juanita is a professional. After doing her homework she knew exactly how to get into the nursing home without creating suspicion."

Frown lines marred Natalie's pretty face. "She must have thought Rod had hidden the money with Gladys. What an evil mind."

There was a lot more he could tell her but not right now. "We're setting up a manhunt to find her. Hopefully it will lead us to her brother. I have to go to headquarters, but I won't leave until the surveillance team gets here. They should be out front any minute."

He picked up the beach ball and rolled it to Amy.

She was so excited she scrambled to her feet to push it toward him. Laughter rolled out of her as they played the game, and it hit him that he loved this little girl. And, heaven help him, he loved her mother, too.

LONG AFTER NATALIE had put Amy down for the night, she still was too wired to go to bed. She changed into pajamas and a robe and went into the den, preferring to watch television on the larger screen. The room was small and could only accommodate the desk and a couch not much bigger than a love seat.

She noticed Kit's bedroll propped in the corner. If he'd tried to sleep on the couch, his feet would have hung over the end. No way would he have gotten any rest. Ever since he'd moved in she'd been worried about him sleeping on the floor, but he never complained.

Tonight he'd gone off without dinner. Those brownies wouldn't hold him for long. She was as bad as a wife who worried about her husband. *But he's not your husband, Natalie.* She could remind herself over and over again, but the fact remained she'd fallen in love with him.

And she had to face another truth. Amy was used to seeing him around the house and had grown attached to him. The longer he stayed here undercover, the more impossible everything was becoming. This wasn't a natural situation.

She needed to discuss it with Kit and decided to wait up for him. A plan had been forming in her mind that seemed to make good sense. Upon her mother's death, Natalie had begun receiving a monthly payment from an annuity. The money automatically went into a Certificate of Deposit to be used for a rainy day. And although Austin was experiencing hot and sunny weather, Natalie's rainy day had come.

She had to do something to free herself and Amy from a situation that was growing more and more untenable. *You're going to be hurt if you don't take action.* Separation was the only answer.

Nothing held her interest on TV, so she reached for a book on Lincoln she'd barely started and made up her mind to get into it. Anything to take her to a different world for a little while.

Near midnight she heard the hum of the garage door lifting and closed her book. Instead of getting up to greet Kit, she stayed on the couch to give him time. In a minute she heard sounds from the kitchen and then she heard him in the hall headed for the guest bathroom. When he walked into the den, the soft light from the lamp made him look grim.

"Kit?"

He lifted his head. "You're still up?"

"I've been waiting for you. Bad night?"

Kit raked his hair, a sign of frustration. "Have you ever gotten up early, ready to get everything done, then realized the people you needed to deal with weren't available yet?"

She nodded. "I know the feeling well."

"That's what it's like for me tonight. All the business I need to do has to wait until tomorrow." He sat on the upholstered chair. "I assumed you'd be asleep by now. What's on your mind?"

"You've got some icing from the brownies on your chin."

He flashed her a quick smile before wiping it off and licking his finger. "Guilty as charged. I finished the last of them."

"Without any dinner?"

"They're better than dinner."

She loved this man with a vengeance. "I can see you're exhausted."

"Not too tired to talk to you. What are you worried about?"

"Our situation."

His eyes narrowed. "I thought it was working just fine."

"It is. You've kept Amy and me perfectly safe, but we don't know how long it's going to take to find those two criminals. You're shackled here in order to protect me. If Juanita Morales was in Denver today, it's not likely they're going to try to break in here again."

"Your point is?" he asked tersely.

She flinched. "You need to be free to conduct that manhunt."

"Explain 'free' to me."

"It's no longer necessary for you to remain here undercover. I realize I still need protection, but that can be done by a private agency that provides bodyguards. I have money in a CD to pay for it. The last thing I want is to deplete your department of officers who have to watch me day and night."

His jaw hardened. "Until this case is solved, the department has an obligation to protect you, so forget dipping into your resources. Is there anything else on your mind?"

"Yes. Amy may only be a toddler, but she's attached to you in a way she never was to Rod. If you're not living here, she'll get over expecting you to walk in the door."

He expelled his breath. "I'll make other arrangements for you tomorrow if you want me to. I'm sorry you're trapped here so she can't play with her little friend across the street. This shouldn't have to go on for too much longer. I also realize you miss your job. Your whole life has been put on hold."

"So has yours, Kit. You're not able to enjoy a private life while you're on a case like mine. But from now on you can go to your own home at night and sleep in your bed instead of on the floor. You must be sick of wearing that clerical shirt. If I were in your shoes, I'd be eager to get rid of it."

While she'd been talking, he'd gotten up to roll out his sleeping bag and pillow. To her surprise he stretched out on top of it still dressed. "You're right. I *am* sick of it. I'm also exhausted."

"I'll leave so you can get some sleep."

"Wait—don't go yet. What about going into a temporary witness protection program with Amy? Would you consider that? You wouldn't have to leave Texas. You'd be removed to a place where you could enjoy a little more freedom but still be kept safe until the threat was over."

Natalie blinked. "Wouldn't the cost of that be more prohibitive than surveillance?"

"Forget the money aspect. Does it appeal to you?"

"No. I'd much rather stay in my home in surroundings that are familiar for Amy. I'm fine here. We both are. You're the one I'm worried about. You've been multitasking, trying to keep us safe and still be a Ranger. You must have eyes in the back of your head."

He chuckled. "That would be a first for the books."

"It's not funny, Kit. If anything happened to you..."

He raised himself up on one elbow and looked searchingly at her. He reached for her arm, gripping it gently. "If anything happened to me...what?"

She could hardly think with him touching her. "I don't want to think about it."

"What don't you want to think about?" he prompted.

Heat enveloped her. "This is a ridiculous conversation."

"You started it," he countered. "What are you afraid of?"

"I—I wouldn't want you to get hurt protecting me." Her stammer was a dead giveaway that her emotions were in turmoil.

"I wouldn't want anything to happen to either of us. For you to get hurt on my watch is unthinkable to me. Come here. Let's talk about it." He pulled her forward until she fell against him on the floor. He gathered her close and entangled their legs.

"Kit—" She half gasped his name.

"On second thought, I don't feel much like talking." He lowered his mouth to hers. Natalie had been wanting this for so long she was past thinking about the wisdom of it. Kit started kissing her with a hunger as great as her own. In an explosion of need she began kissing him back, forgetting everything as she poured out her feelings for him.

One kiss turned into another until she was trembling with desire. His hands and his mouth fueled the fire that was licking through her body. She'd never known rapture like this.

"I'm sorry, Natalie. I've tried to keep my distance, but it isn't possible. I want you—you have no idea how much." He buried his face in her neck.

"I feel the same way, but I was afraid you might be too chivalrous to kiss me, even if you found yourself wanting to."

He groaned and brought his face back to hers, kissing her until she hardly knew herself. "I've been denying myself since the day we met," he confessed against her lips. "It's been hell."

She no longer had to wonder what it would be like to lie in this Texas Ranger's arms. When she felt able to take a breath she said, "That night in the car outside the motel, I wanted so badly to let you know how I felt about you, but I was afraid you might not feel the same way."

Whatever he would have said was silenced by the ringing of his cell phone. Afraid of what it meant, she eased away from him so he could answer it.

"Cy, what's going on?" The Ranger wouldn't be calling him at one in the morning without a good reason.

Natalie felt Kit's body tense and knew he'd just been given some important news. When he ended the call, he wasn't the same amorous man who'd been kissing the daylights out of her. In an instant he'd turned back into the Ranger.

"I have to go to headquarters," he stated. "A surveillance team will be here in a few minutes."

Natalie got to her feet, knowing better than to badger him with questions. While he got ready, she went into the kitchen and packed up a couple of sandwiches for him to take. They met at the door leading into the garage. He'd put on his tan shirt and badge. "The guys are out in front, so you're in good hands."

She nodded and handed him the sack. "You need food to keep you going."

"Thank you, but I hope you know I need this more." He put his hand behind her head and kissed her until she was swaying. "I'll be in touch with you tomorrow."

"Whatever is going on, good luck, Kit."

Natalie locked up behind him and hurried through the house to the front window to watch him drive away, taking her heart with him.

Chapter Eight

Kit had told Natalie he was going into headquarters, but he planned to meet Cy at the jail.

Thanks to some fine investigating by the Colorado police after Kit had told them about Julia Varoz, they'd gotten a tip from the secretary working for Dr. Nyman. She'd met Ms. Varoz when she'd come into the doctor's office on Friday morning wanting an appointment.

When told he was on vacation, she'd left the office and said she'd be back. The secretary had followed her out to get something from her own car and noticed the woman drive off in a new black Lexus.

When the APB went out, some Texas patrolmen had spotted her Lexus and stopped her on the highway inside the Texas border. They'd arrested her on multiple counts of impersonating a doctor, fleeing arrest on the mortgage fraud scheme, murdering Harold Park and possession of fake IDs.

Overjoyed there was only one killer left at large before Natalie's case could be closed, Kit drove to the jail munching one of the ham sandwiches she'd made for him. Cy was waiting for him in the parking lot. He got out of the car.

"You did it, bud. You found her."

They walked inside. "Not me. Natalie. She was inspired to ask if there were pictures taken at the service for Gladys. In fact she's been inspired all the way along."

"But you were the one who flew her to Denver in the first place and got that information on Salter."

"Either way, we still have to find Alonzo."

"Maybe if we interrogate Juanita together, she'll crack."

"It's worth a try. This is a big win."

"I bet the boss even smiled when he heard about her arrest."

They passed through the checkpoint and walked down a corridor to the interrogation room. The guard at the door nodded to them.

"We're here to question the prisoner." They showed their IDs.

"You're on the list." He opened the door. Another guard stood inside.

Juanita, in striped prison garb, sat on the far side of the table. Her hands and ankles were shackled. She was thirty-two years of age but looked older, harder, than the mug shot taken eight years ago. The blond wig was missing. Her black hair hung loose to her shoulders and Kit noticed she'd had a recent manicure. Purple nails.

She sat back in the chair with her chin held high. "Ooh—two Texas Rangers." Her dark eyes flashed and she said something vulgar.

Kit went first. "Your bad mouth won't get you any-where, Juanita."

"I'm not talking!"

His brows lifted. "You might care *if* you cooper-ate. You and your brother, Alonzo, are wanted for the murder of Harold Park. If Alonzo pulled the trigger in-stead of you, it could shorten the length of your prison sentence."

She eyed him with defiance. "Sure it could."

"You're the one with the problem, not me. Are you waiting for Marcos to get out of prison? Is that why you wanted to steal the four-hundred thousand from Park, so you can pay off the bill Marcos owes? Is he your lover? We've got you on a security tape at the Austin airport parking with Park. Was he your lover before you turned on him?"

No response.

Cy started in. "That was quite a haul you made from the dummy mortgage company. Twenty-eight-million dollars—that must be how you paid for the Lexus you were driving. It's going to lead us to your brother, but if you want to give us some help, it could buy you less time in prison. Think about it."

Juanita remained cool and collected. They weren't going to get anything out of her. By tacit agreement Kit and Cy left the interrogation room and headed for the exit.

"Do you think she'll consider your offer?"

Kit shook his head. "I don't know. Let's see how another twelve hours in jail affects her."

When they reached Kit's car, Cy said, "How's it going with Natalie?"

"Funny you should ask."

"Uh, oh."

Kit threw his head back. "She told me it was time for me to go. As if I didn't already know."

"What was her reason?"

"She said Amy was growing too attached to me."

"That's no surprise. What are you going to do?"

"I've got the surveillance crew guarding her 24/7. Do you know she offered to use her own money to hire a private bodyguard service to spare the department's budget?"

"As Luckey said, she's nice, in all the ways that count. Beautiful, too."

"Yup."

"I'm going to go home and get some shut-eye. How about you?"

"The same. I haven't been to my condo in over a week. See you in the morning. We've got a lot of work to do."

"You can say that again."

They parted company and Kit headed for his condo, finishing his other sandwich on the way. When he arrived at his place, he was pleased to see that his cleaning lady had kept it dust free. Once he'd grabbed a quick shower he climbed into bed and set his watch alarm for 7:00 a.m., then turned onto his stomach. Lying on a mattress definitely beat sleeping on the floor, but it didn't feel right being alone.

The place felt empty. There weren't any warm bodies in the house with him. No chance of stepping on a beach ball or a cow. No out-of-this-world brownies sitting on the kitchen counter begging to be eaten. No sweet-smelling female waiting for him on the couch. No little angel calling out his name, holding up her hands to be hugged and kissed.

Natalie had been right to suggest a change in their arrangement. Tonight he'd wanted her so badly there would have been no stopping him if Cy hadn't phoned when he had. Letting go of her was the hardest thing he'd ever had to do.

What kind of a Ranger was he to take advantage of the woman he'd promised to keep safe? It didn't matter that she'd responded with the same hunger that drove him. He should have been the one in control. Until he closed the case, he didn't have the right to stay at her house overnight.

Tonight he'd taken off the clerical shirt and wouldn't be putting it on again. Father Segal was no more and already Kit felt as if he was in mourning.

WHEN KIT CAME to the next morning, he realized he'd slept through his alarm. It was eight-thirty. After a quick shave, he dressed in jeans and a shirt. Attaching his badge to the pocket, he left the condo. En route to headquarters he grabbed breakfast at a drive-through.

Cy was already at his desk as Kit walked by. "You're as late as I am. TJ has called a meeting for nine."

"That gives me five minutes." Kit went into his office to phone Natalie. She'd be up by now. He wouldn't be able to get through the day until he'd talked to her. She answered on the second ring.

"Kit?"

"Good morning. How did you sleep?"

"Fine. You must have loved being in your bed."

"I did. Listen, I'll be by later today to get all my things, but I'll phone you when I'm on my way. How's the cherub?"

"She's in her high chair making a big mess of her breakfast."

He chuckled. "Sounds like she's in top form." Natalie didn't mention whether she'd asked for him, and he resisted inquiring. "Thanks for those sandwiches. They saved my life last night. I discovered that no matter how delicious they are, man can't live on brownies alone."

She let out a little laugh. "Are you at work?"

"Yes. I'm about to go into a big meeting with the boss." He refrained from telling her to give Amy a hug from him. "Have a good day, Natalie. If you need me for any reason, just call."

"I'll remember. Stay safe, Ranger Saunders."

He hung up, not liking the formality. If what had happened between them last night was an aberration on her part, he didn't want to know about it. He'd left her house with an ache that had stayed with him, and she was the only person who could take it away.

Half a dozen Rangers were seated in TJ's office when he walked in. Cy had already arrived. Kit took a place next to Ranger Rodriguez.

"I've assembled you men to brief you on our manhunt for Alonzo Morales, responsible for the twenty-eight-million-dollar mortgage fraud that stole funds from nine banks. He's been on the Most Wanted list for eight years.

"Due to the brilliant work of Rangers Saunders and Vance, Morales's sister, Juanita, a known felon also on the Most Wanted list, was arrested last night driving to Austin from Denver. We're convinced that either she or Alonzo killed Harold Park, but she's not talking, having worked two cons—the Empire mortgage fraud case and the LifeSpan accounting fraud case.

"We believe Morales is in the Austin area searching for the four-hundred-thousand dollars, a percentage of the eight million embezzled by Park that's missing from the pharmaceutical corporation. We have to assume that he's armed and dangerous.

"You've all been given photos and rap sheets. His pictures are everywhere in Texas as well as the western states. Stay alert and report anything you hear to me, Saunders or Vance. That's all."

Everyone filed out except Kit.

"Captain? I wanted to inform you that I'm no longer staying at the Harris home undercover. Now that Juanita is jailed, one danger has been removed. So I'm having Mrs. Harris guarded outside the house by around-the-clock surveillance until we catch Morales."

"Smart move to free yourself up," TJ responded.

Kit averted his eyes. "Yes, sir."

Kit left the room to go back to his office. He needed to talk to the attorney in charge of Gladys Park's finances. If by any chance Harold had been in touch with his grandmother before his death, Kit would find out. He also wanted the attorney to know Gladys had a living relative, little Amy Harris.

When he reached the office of Farbes and Lowell and told the secretary he was calling on behalf of the Texas Rangers, Mr. Farbes came right on the line.

After Kit explained his business, the man sounded shocked. "You mean to tell me Harold Park married and had a child?"

"Yes."

"This is amazing. Joseph Park was a very successful architect and kept a considerable sum of money in trust, which he left to his wife. After his death she drew up her own will. Upon her death she asked that any money was to pass to their descendants or, in the absence of any living descendants, to their favorite charity.

"Since Harold was never found, my offices were preparing that charitable donation, but it hasn't yet taken place. I would need to fly to Austin and meet the mother of Harold's child. Depending on verification of birth records, that money could be put in trust for her."

Excitement for Natalie swept through Kit. "I'll email you all the pertinent information after we get off the phone. How soon can Mrs. Harris expect to hear from you?"

"I'll contact her within the week, Ranger Saunders."

"Thank you. She'll be waiting for your call."

Kit hung up, dazed by the turn of events. He couldn't wait to tell Natalie.

After he sent the necessary documentation to the attorney, he phoned Natalie and explained he was coming over to pick up his bedroll and toiletries.

On his way out the door he received a call from the circuit servant for the Kingdom Hall area. The two women who'd come to Natalie's door were indeed Jehovah Witnesses and had been passing out their literature in her neighborhood. Both the lawn service man and the missionaries had been legitimate. Kit could cross them off his list of persons of interest.

NATALIE WAS NERVOUS about seeing Kit again so soon. It was only eleven. She'd told him she'd slept fine, but that was a lie. She'd been awake most of the night and wished she hadn't suggested that he go back to his house. The need to be in his arms was causing her physical pain.

Amy had babbled about him all morning. If she saw him, she'd want to play. Natalie couldn't allow that to happen and put her down for a short nap. After a protest, she finally fell asleep.

Natalie showered and dressed in a skirt and blouse. After brushing her hair she put on a little more makeup than usual to conceal the fatigue lines. She didn't want him to think she expected a repeat of last night, in case he was regretting the lapse. But the truth was it downright frightened her, the possibility he might never kiss her again.

While she made fresh coffee, Natalie reasoned that she knew he wasn't a man who played women. But what kind of a message had she been sending him, waiting up for him as she had last night? No doubt he could sense how crazy she was about him—subconsciously she'd wanted it to happen. Any normal man would have made a pass, even a highly principled Texas Ranger. But she'd been so embarrassingly eager in her response...

The sound of the garage door lifting was music to her ears. Her cheeks felt hot just knowing he was here. When Kit walked in, she stayed busy emptying the dishwasher. "Hello, stranger," she teased without looking at him. "Long time no see."

"It seems like eons," he drawled in his deep voice, sending ripples of delight through her. "I've come with some amazing news."

She wheeled around and got caught in his all-encompassing gaze. "You've captured Alonzo Morales?"

"I wish that were the case. This is something else that directly affects you. Where's Amy?"

"Taking a nap."

"Then why don't we sit down."

Her heart thudded. "All right. Would you like coffee? I'm going to have some."

"That sounds good."

In her nervousness she spilled some of the hot liquid as she poured it into the mugs. After wiping up, she added cream and sugar and took them to the table. He held the chair out for her then sat across from her.

No more priest's collar. The formality was killing her.

"Thanks for the coffee. This is what I've needed all morning." He sipped the hot brew. "All right. Today I had a talk with Mr. Farbes, the attorney who handled the affairs of Gladys and Joseph Park. He was very interested to learn that the Parks have a living relative in Amy, and he will be contacting you and setting up a time to meet."

The mug almost slipped out of her hand. "Are you talking about an inheritance?"

"Yes. I have no idea of the amount, but he did say that Joseph Park was very successful in his profession. I'm sure he'll answer all your questions, but I wanted to tell you now so his phone call doesn't surprise you. Now, if you'll excuse me, I'll gather my things."

In a stupor-like state Natalie finished her coffee. It didn't take Kit long to appear with his arms loaded. He went out to his car and came back in empty-handed.

She looked up at him, feeling the wrench of loss. He'd only been here temporarily, but her soul was already grieving to know he wouldn't be staying with her anymore. "Again I find myself thanking you for everything. I never would have thought to inquire about Gladys's financial situation.

"I keep thinking back to the graveside service. I was in a state of shock, but not for long because one of the legendary Texas Rangers came to my rescue and restored my world in a brand-new way. Don't say you were just doing your job. I don't want to hear it."

His expression remained solemn as he responded. "I'll text you every day to keep you informed about your case. I have every reason to expect we'll catch Morales before the week is out. Then you can get back to work and Amy can go back to playing with her little friend across the street."

A text? He didn't even want to hear her voice? She supposed it was the perfect way for him to keep feelings and emotions out of the conversation. Perhaps he didn't regret last night, but he was backing away so she wouldn't get any ideas about it happening again.

"What about the camera at the front door?"

"We'll leave it for now. There's a chance it could still provide us with a clue. For the time being I'll keep the key and the remote."

But you won't use it, her heart cried.

"Thanks again for the coffee. Enjoy your day and don't worry. The arrests of Marcos and Juanita have been made public. The news is everywhere, so we can be pretty sure Alonzo will hear about it and make a mistake. When he does, we're ready for him."

Kit disappeared too quickly for her to say anything else. She had the crazy urge to run after him, but what good would it do to chase him? It would be too painful and humiliating. Apparently he'd quit her cold turkey and it was all her fault.

She went to her bedroom and changed into a pair of shorts and a T-shirt. Amy would be up soon and she would take her out to play in the backyard.

As she dressed Amy for play time, Natalie decided she would also take her laptop out to the patio table and pay bills. It would help fill her day.

When it was nearly time to go in for lunch, Natalie's phone rang. It was a Colorado area code.

"Hello?"

"Mrs. Harris? This is John Farbes from Farbes and Lowell in Denver. We represent the estate of Gladys Park."

"Oh, yes. Ranger Saunders told me you'd be calling."

"Would it be possible for me to come to your home at noon tomorrow to speak with you about your daughter?"

"That would be fine."

"He told you the reason?"

"He did, yes."

"Good. I'll see you soon, then." The attorney confirmed Natalie's address and suggested some of the documents she might want to have on hand for their meeting. "Thank you, Mrs. Harris."

"Thank *you*."

KEEP BUSY OR GO CRAZY.

Kit swung by the grocery store to do some shopping. Then he drove to his condo to put everything away. His sandwiches didn't taste like Natalie's. He drank half a quart of milk. Still not satisfied, he reached for the pack of chocolate-chip cookies. As he was opening it, his cell rang. The government number on the ID could mean several things.

"Ranger Saunders speaking."

"This is Officer Walton at the jail. Juanita Morales's arraignment before the judge is scheduled for three o'clock. She's asked to speak to you first. Alone."

Well, well, well. It sounded as if she was getting nervous. That was a good sign and worth his trouble to find out what she wanted before she headed to the courthouse.

A half hour later it was like déjà vu as he entered the interrogation room. He turned on his digital recorder.

Juanita didn't display the attitude of the day before. Overnight she'd lost her confidence and looked pitiful in her shackles.

"You're going to be taken before the judge within the hour. Say what you have to say."

This time her eyes didn't flash. They looked dull. "Did you mean what you said about cutting time off my sentence if I give you information?"

"That depends on how valuable it is."

"Harold's wife is in danger."

Her statement burned like acid. "What makes you say that?"

"Alonzo and I were the ones who ransacked her house."

"What were you looking for?"

"Four-hundred-thousand dollars and two guns. My brother was sure they were there, but we found nothing."

That money has to be somewhere. "Tell me where he put the millions he helped Marcos embezzle from nine banks."

"He lost most of it on bad investments and gambling."

"Were you involved with Marcos?"

"No. I hated him." That came as a surprise. "My brother should never have gotten mixed up with him."

"How did they meet?"

"My fault. I had a boyfriend in Denver who was an accountant. I learned a lot from him. When my brother said he had a plan to escape prison if I helped him, I couldn't turn him down. Our parents died early and he kept me alive. This was my way to pay him back. I drove him and Harold to Texas. When we got there, I needed a job.

"Marcos advertised for an accountant. I applied and he hired me. Before long I could see what he was doing and wanted to leave. He threatened to kill me if I didn't do what he wanted. By then he knew my brother was an escaped felon. They both used me."

"Tell me something I don't know."

"I didn't kill Harold. I've never killed anyone." The hard as nails woman teared up. Somehow Kit believed her. "My brother was furious because Harold had double-crossed him. Alonzo was the one who had the plan to escape eight years ago. He thought he could trust Harold. My brother put a gun to his head and gave him one last chance to tell him where the money was hidden before he blew his brains out.

"Harold swore it was in the house, hidden in a place no one would think to look for it.

"Alonzo called him a liar. My brother always did have a violent temper and he shot Harold just as he was about to tell him where to look. After we left the hotel he ordered me to go to Denver to find out if Harold had hidden the money with his grandmother. Alonzo needed that money to pay some gambling debts and he said if I didn't go, he'd kill me."

Kit checked his digital recorder to make certain everything was getting picked up. So far, so good. He looked at Juanita.

"Where did he hang out?"

"With friends in the back of Raul's Billiards in Round Rock. I'm sure he's not there now." No, but it could give Kit a lead. "It took time to come up with a plan, but it put space between me and the police who were looking for me after Marcos was arrested." She grimaced. "It was a wasted trip. Harold's grandmother told me her life story, but there was no mention of the money."

"Why did you go to her funeral service?"

"How do you know about that?"

"I have my ways." Thanks to Natalie.

"I thought maybe I'd hear the pastor say something in passing about her belongings and where they'd been stored, but no such luck. I called my brother and told him.

"That's when he said he was going back to Harold's house, and he said that if Harold's wife got in his way, he would kill her to get the money."

Kit's blood ran cold. He got to his feet while she was still speaking.

"That trip has put me in this hellhole. My brother won't come to my rescue because I know too much now. After he finds the money, he'll bribe someone to kill me in prison."

Kit exhaled sharply. "I'll see what I can do."

He left the jail at a dead run. The second he got in the car he phoned Cy at headquarters. "Hey, bud. Big break in the case. I'll explain after I've picked you up.

Wait for me at the entrance to the underground parking. I should be there in five minutes."

After ringing off, he phoned TJ and told him about Juanita's confession. "I'm headed for Natalie's to take her and Amy to my condo. I'm taking Cy with me to set a trap." He would hide Cy in the back of his car.

"I'll send a surveillance crew to your condo."

"Will you also call Judge Leemaster? Tell him I have the recording of Juanita's confession. She wasn't the killer. I want him to keep that in mind."

The proof on his digital recorder ought to persuade the judge to give Juanita some kind of break, no matter how small. When she'd talked about her brother, he'd seen real fear. The details of their childhood would probably be a horror story he wouldn't wish on anyone.

"Consider it done. And, Kit? Watch your back."

"I intend to."

Chapter Nine

Natalie had just started a wash when she heard noises from the nursery. Amy had awakened from her nap and wanted out of the crib. At the same time she received a text on her phone and her heart leaped. Driving into the garage.

Kit had come again when she'd least expected it. He entered the kitchen like a man on a mission, his piercing gaze zeroing in on her. "Quick! I need to get you and Amy out of the house *now*. I'll explain later. Cy is with me. He's putting the car seat in my car. While you get Amy ready, I'll load the playpen, the high chair and a few other things you might need."

Within five minutes the three of them had gathered the most important items and clothes and put them in the trunk of Kit's car. Amy called Kit's name and he paused long enough to kiss her before settling her into her car seat with some of her favorite stuffed animals.

While the two Rangers went back into the house, Natalie sat next to her daughter to comfort her. "Kit will be right back. We're going on an adventure," she said, trying to calm her own pounding heart. They had to be in grave danger for him to burst into the house the way he had.

When he came out to the car, he was alone. He pressed the remote, then backed out onto the street. She noticed that the surveillance van had gone.

Kit talked Ranger business on his phone as he drove. Wherever he was taking them she'd find out when they got there. Amy chattered the whole time, excited to be doing something different. Without Kit around, Natalie realized she and her daughter had been going stir crazy in the house.

"We're home," Kit announced. They'd come to the area called Chimney Corners, not far from where Natalie lived. He pulled into the driveway of a town-house condo complex and drove into the garage.

They entered one of the units through the kitchen where he deposited the high chair. As he helped her get her things inside, she looked around the living room, spying some framed pictures of Kit and his family on the end tables. He'd brought them to his home. She'd wondered where he lived, never expecting to see the inside of it.

He set up the playpen so she could deposit Amy with some toys. "For the time being she can sleep in the playpen while you sleep on the couch. It's amazingly comfortable, I promise. I'll get you sheets and quilts. I'm afraid I only have two bedrooms upstairs and I use one as my office. It's a small place, but perfect for me until I buy a home with horse property."

She darted him a glance. "You think we might have to be here for a while?"

"I can't predict." He disappeared up the stairs and brought down bedding and pillows. "You can use the bathroom near the foot of the stairs. The fridge is stocked, so feel free to help yourself to anything."

Natalie took Amy's snacks and jars of baby food into the kitchen. Before long everything had been organized.

She went back to the living room where she found Kit playing with Amy. He'd taken her out of the playpen and was stacking blocks with her. The little girl loved the attention of the tall, handsome Ranger.

So do I, Natalie thought.

"Can you tell me what's going on now, Kit?"

He looked over his shoulder before gravitating to one of the chairs. "I was called into the jail earlier. Juanita decided she wanted to make her confession in the hope the judge would go a little easier on her. She explained that her brother killed your husband because he'd double-crossed him."

"That was your theory all along."

"The confession substantiated it, but my blood chilled when she said Alonzo is convinced the money is still hidden in your house, and that he's willing to kill you in order to get to it. Because Juanita's arrest was publicized, she's certain he'll go back for it any time now."

Natalie felt a shiver run down her spine.

"While you're here, a surveillance crew will remain outside the condo for your safety. Cy will be at the house, waiting for Alonzo to break in, no matter how long it takes."

"I'm sure Juanita's brother isn't working alone."

"You let me worry about that."

She sucked in her breath. "Won't he see you letting yourself into my house?"

"That's not the plan. One of the guys will drive a car with a real estate logo and put up a For Sale sign in your front yard with a number to call. After he leaves, we're hoping Alonzo will think you've been frightened off. Believing that the house is vacant, he'll come for the money. The ruse might work, but it might not. In any case Cy will be inside waiting for him. I'll provide backup."

"Where will you be?"

"In the big tree growing in the backyard on your neighbor's property. On the first day I came to your house through the back, I noticed it would provide the perfect perch."

Oh, Kit...

She opened the Little People Farm that Kit had grabbed for her to bring. Amy loved it and started arranging all the animals.

"I need your cell to call Mr. Farbes. He'll have to put off his visit until Alonzo is captured."

Natalie had forgotten all about the attorney. She reached for her purse and handed him the phone. While they talked, she got up and went into the kitchen to put some milk in Amy's sippy cup in case she was thirsty. As she turned to go back to the living room with it, Kit was right there.

"Oh—sorry. I didn't see you." She would have run into him if he hadn't steadied her shoulders with his hands. The contact shot darts of awareness through her body. "How did Mr. Farbes take the news?" She could hear her voice shaking.

Kit's hands moved to her upper arms. He squeezed them before letting her go. Natalie wished he hadn't touched her. "He'll be happy to come when this nightmare is over."

"I'm so glad you remembered." She moved past him and returned to the living room. Amy saw her and raised her hands. "Mik."

Kit was right behind her. "Milk," he said back. "That was almost perfect, Amy."

"As you've noticed, *L*'s and *H*'s are hard for her." Natalie handed her the cup and sat on the floor next to her. Her pulse raced when Kit stretched out on the floor, too. His hard, lean body was too close.

With one hand propping up his head, he teased Amy by taking her animals away one at a time. When she grabbed one from him, he reached for another. They played back and forth until he had her giggling uncontrollably and she dropped the cup she'd been holding.

"I don't believe my daughter has ever had this much fun."

When he flicked his gaze to her, his eyes danced. "I haven't, either. I know we planned to distance ourselves, but circumstances have thrown us together again and I find this little cherub to be excellent company."

"If she could say the words, she'd tell you the same thing." Natalie was starting to feel emotional. "Kit—

thank you for getting us out of harm's way. Your whole life has been upended because of me."

He grasped the hand closest to him and kissed her palm. The action was so intimate she could hardly breathe. "I like being upended. These are the perks of being a Ranger. You never know what your next case will bring.

"When I went to the cemetery to take pictures, I didn't like the fact that I was attracted to you even before we'd met. I knew you were a person of interest to the police, but I found myself not wanting you to be guilty of a crime. Someone else should have worked this case instead of me, but the pull you had on me overruled my good sense. When I told the boss my plan, he had reservations about it, but he didn't try to stop me."

She averted her eyes. "I'm afraid my good sense failed me when you gave me the choice between having the surveillance team watching me or having you guard me yourself. I liked the idea of my cousin Todd visiting me for the week. But I was thinking selfishly and didn't consider that Amy could be affected."

"She may be little, but she exudes her own personality."

"She definitely does. You asked me if I thought she'd be disturbed to see a strange man in the house. I didn't have to think about it because…because I sensed the goodness in you. So did she."

He reached for Amy and held her in the air while he was on his back. "Do you want to swim?" He moved her like she was a fish.

"Swim!" she echoed, loving this new game.

"That's right, sweetheart. Swim, swim."

When he put her down, she protested.

"Do you want to swim again?"

"Swim gain."

"Did you hear that, Mommy? She said she wants to swim again. She's speaking in sentences. I knew you were a smart girl." He moved her around some more, dipping her near Natalie several times. The giggling continued.

By now Natalie was laughing along with Kit. She couldn't imagine heaven being more wonderful than this. *Make it last*, her heart cried. But of course it couldn't because he'd be leaving when it got dark to face a known killer.

Forcing herself to bring things to an end she said, "It's time for your dinner, Amy. I bet you're hungry after that workout. Let's get your diaper changed first." She got up from the floor and reached for her daughter. The bathroom counter would be a good place for that.

"'Bye, Amy," Kit said, still lying down.

"Bye-bye."

Natalie took her into the bathroom. She put a towel down then reached into the diaper bag for a Pamper. Soon her daughter was ready. She carried her to the kitchen and put her in the high chair. After washing her hands, she reached for a jar of noodles and turkey and selected peaches for dessert.

Kit came in a few minutes later. "Feel like breakfast for dinner?"

"Always," she answered.

"I make a Texas omelet almost as good as your brownies. Even my mom says they're better than hers."

"That's because you learned from her."

"Yup. It's about the only thing I cooked that I didn't ruin."

"I had a few disasters myself growing up."

They bantered throughout the delicious meal, exchanging life stories. While they ate, Amy found her little shopping cart in the living room and pushed it into the kitchen, purposely running into Kit's chair. He'd spoiled her so much she was wearing herself out with excitement. Natalie figured her little girl would fall into a deep sleep once she put her down. It was growing late.

Kit insisted on doing the dishes, so Natalie went into the living room to empty the playpen and lay out a quilt for Amy. After putting her in her footed pajamas, she lowered her into the playpen and handed her the cow she treasured.

"Nite, nite." She kissed the top of her head.

Amy didn't like being put down. She stood at the railing. "Kit—" she called out in a loud voice. It sounded so urgent, Natalie burst into laughter. He came running.

"I think she wants you to say good-night."

He hunkered down in front of the playpen. "It's time to go to sleep, sweetheart. Nite, nite."

All of a sudden the tears came. Amy stood there not knowing what to do with herself. "Mama—Kit—"

"I'd better go back to the kitchen," he whispered.

One more kiss to the top of her head and he left the

living room, already bathed in darkness. Amy whimpered for a few minutes then sank down. Natalie sang a couple of songs she loved. Pretty soon silence reigned. The little girl had finally fallen asleep.

Natalie made up the couch for bed. Kit had brought down sheets designed with Texas Longhorn steers. She loved them. His mother had probably put sheets like these on his bed when he was a boy.

Natalie had liked Kit's mother very much during the short time they'd had to talk at the rodeo. The pride over her sons had shone in her eyes. Who wouldn't be proud? Kit was in a class of his own.

With everything done except to put on her pajamas, she walked into the spotless kitchen and found Kit on the phone. He spoke in low tones so she couldn't make out the words. He was probably talking to Cy.

How they handled what they did for a living was beyond Natalie's ability to comprehend. But she was incredibly thankful for men like him, and she couldn't imagine him doing anything else.

Being a Ranger was part of who he was. Natalie was fiercely glad of it. She loved him with her whole being. No matter how risky life was for him every day, she wouldn't want him any other way.

She could tell the moment he ended his call that he was preparing himself to leave. She grasped the back of one of the kitchen chairs. "Is it time?"

"Afraid so." He got up from his chair and turned to her. His features looked chiseled in the semi darkness.

"Go get him, cowboy."

"I intend to." The fierce tone in his voice had a

heart-stopping effect on her. "How about a kiss for luck?"

She struggled for breath. "You don't need any but I might, so I'll kiss you anyway."

She moved toward him and put her hands on his well-defined chest. He was letting her do all the work. That didn't matter. She wanted to let him know how she felt and slid her arms up around his neck. Natalie had to rise on her toes to give him the kind of kiss she was dying for.

The world spun away as he crushed her in his arms and gave her a devouring kiss she would never forget. It said so many things they hadn't yet spoken to each other, but she didn't need a translator to tell her what she'd prayed would happen. As Colette had told her a week ago, it was there in his eyes and in his body language.

Her heartbeat merged with his. Their bodies molded together in one singing line of desire. Words weren't necessary; not when they were communing in the age-old way that brought bodies and souls to life. This magnificent Ranger made her feel immortal.

They'd only known each other a short time, but something so incredible had happened to her she knew his hold over her would last forever. There'd been such darkness in her marriage. Yet Kit had brought the light back into her life, the glory of being loved and cherished. Those were elements she'd never known before from any man and never would again. If she couldn't have Kit, she didn't want anyone else.

Aching with love, she cupped his face in her hands.

"Come home soon, Ranger Saunders. You're needed by an awful lot of people."

Natalie made a swift exit from Kit's arms and hurried into the living room.

THAT KISS HAD fanned the flame burning inside him. On fire with near-white heat, he'd left his condo and headed for her house.

Come on, Morales. Bring it on.

He parked his car one street over as he'd done that first night. He put his night-vision goggles around his neck. No one was in sight. He locked the car and darted through several yards. There were a number of fences to scale before he reached the tree in question. He'd done a lot of tree climbing in his youth. This one was easy.

When he reached midway and was well hidden by leaves, he phoned Cy.

"Where are you?"

"In the tree looking at the back of the house. Have the guys put up the sign?"

"About an hour ago."

"Good. I take it there's been no other movement."

"Not yet."

"In that case, I'm going to join you. Leave the back door open. I'll be there in two minutes." He disconnected and started down the tree. One more fence to climb and he'd be there.

When he crept in through the back door, it felt like home.

Cy was waiting for him in the kitchen.

Kit smiled. "Good to see you, bud."

"Likewise. Guess who else is here?"

Kit couldn't imagine.

"Vic."

"You're kidding—"

"Nope. After you gave me the tip from Juanita about Alonzo hiding out at the billiards place, I went over there to investigate. One of the girls who works at the front as cashier is terrified of him and hopes we get him. She said he always has two thugs with him and carries an AR-15. They operate like a gang and drive around in an old hearse.

"When Vic heard that, he volunteered to help us on this stakeout. There's a bulletproof vest for you on the chair there. Needless to say the boss wants this killer caught."

Good old TJ.

Kit put on the vest, then walked through the house feeling a ton heavier. He found Vic in Natalie's bedroom watching the windows through his night-vision goggles. They talked shop for a few minutes before Kit returned to the kitchen.

Cy eyed him. "What's your gut telling you, Kit?"

"The way Juanita explained it, I figure it's going to go down gangster style. She says Alonzo's a raging bull and he's got nothing to lose at this point. I have no doubt he'll blast his way in.

"The only problem is, I don't know how long we're going to have to wait. Juanita felt it would happen right away because he's desperate to settle his gambling debts. I hate tying up Vic when this isn't even his case."

"He insisted, and the boss knows we work well together. He'll send other guys to relieve us tomorrow if it looks like we'll have to be here longer."

Kit nodded and pulled out his weapon. "Which door do you want to guard?"

"Doesn't matter."

"I'll take the front and you cover the back. We'll trade off." Kit had a hunch they'd charge the front of the house and shoot the door off its hinges. Of course, anything was possible. He placed himself to the side of the glass so he could see the whole front yard.

His father had gotten into a situation like this. But the shootout had taken his life. Kit wasn't ready for that to happen yet. Tonight he'd found a new reason for wanting to live life to its fullest. Natalie may not have said all the words he wanted to hear, but he knew how she felt about him.

Go get him, cowboy.

Those were magic words. They'd freed him from the fear that she couldn't handle what he did for a living. During all the years since he and Janie had broken up, he'd been afraid to fall in love. He couldn't go through that again, only to be told that his career was getting in the way of total fulfillment.

Kit had seen how hard it had been on Luckey. The poor guy had suffered when his wife had said goodbye. To be told that you had to find a different way to make a living after a year of marriage would have been devastating. Luckey was doing better, but he was as gun shy about falling in love again as Kit had been.

Tonight Kit had been given a gift he hadn't expected. He didn't have to worry about that issue with Natalie. Even though she knew his father had been killed in the line of duty, she'd sent him off with her heart in her eyes, willing him to come back to her. That's what he intended to do. He could see a future opening up. A fantastic future with the cherub and, God willing, maybe even a few more.

While he kept watch, he checked in with the guys on his phone. Maybe tonight wouldn't be the night. Only a few cars had gone by. They talked strategies. The hours dragged on. He ate a couple of Snickers.

Around three-thirty in the morning when Kit had just about decided it wasn't going to happen, he saw a dark vehicle turn onto the street and park a few houses away on the opposite side.

He alerted the guys to get ready.

Three figures had gotten out and were creeping toward the house. No sooner had Kit warned his buddies than the front window shattered from the impact of a semi-automatic weapon, just as Kit had imagined. Shards of glass flew in all directions. With his adrenaline gushing, he waited against the wall until they started to climb inside.

Kit aimed his gun and shot the first two thugs. He would never forget the look of shock on Alonzo's face as he spun around in the moonlight before falling to the floor. Cy shot at the third intruder, but he turned and started running.

"Oh, no, you don't." Kit climbed up on the window sill and jumped to the grass. The thug shot at him, then took off toward the car. Kit raced after him and tackled him before he could open the door. It was like throwing a steer; the guy fell hard against the pavement and lost consciousness. With a grunt of satisfaction, Kit reached into his pocket to pull out his cuffs when a fourth man pointed a gun at him through the open rear window of the car. Kit hadn't counted on him.

"Get down!" Cy yelled. Kit had already obeyed the instinct and heard two shots fired. The last thing he remembered was a stinging sensation in his upper right arm.

NATALIE WOKE at seven and looked over at Amy. She was still asleep, her knees pulled up beneath her and her cute little bottom in the air. Her quilt was wrapped around her middle. It was a hilarious site. She quickly grabbed her phone and took a picture. Kit would laugh his head off.

Her body quickened when she thought of him. She had no idea how long it would be before she spoke to him again, let alone saw him. But it didn't matter because however long it took, she knew he'd eventually come home and she'd be here waiting for him.

While Amy was still out cold, Natalie got dressed in a pair of jeans and a blouse. After freshening up in the bathroom she went into the kitchen to make coffee. Just as she found the jar of decaf in the cupboard, she heard the phone ring. Her heart pounded. Maybe it was Kit.

She answered.

"Mrs. Harris? This is Milo, one of the surveillance crew out front. You're going to have a visitor in a minute. It's Ranger Saunders's mother. I didn't want you to be startled."

Kit's mother? "Thank you for letting me know."

"You're welcome."

She hung up, curious to know why the older woman had come. Kit's mother was probably here for an unannounced visit and would no doubt be surprised to find Natalie in residence. She was glad she'd gotten up and dressed.

She walked to the front door and opened it in time to see Kit's mother walking toward her. She was dressed in jeans and a top much like Natalie was wearing, but the older woman looked paler than Natalie remembered and for some reason she started to get nervous. "Mrs. Saunders?"

The woman's hazel eyes looked at Natalie for an overly long moment. "There's no way to make this easy for you, Natalie." Natalie's heart plummeted. "Kit was injured last night. His captain asked me to come over here because he knew Kit had brought you here and that you'd need to be told."

She gasped. "But he's still alive. Right?"

"Yes. By some miracle he is."

Natalie felt weakness overtake her as if she might faint, but she'd never fainted in her life. "Come in and tell me what happened."

"Oh. Your little girl is still asleep," Mrs. Saunders said quietly as they entered the living room.

"It's fine. Please. Sit down."

"I've just come from the hospital. I don't know all the facts yet, but he got shot in his upper arm."

"Oh, no—" Natalie exclaimed, causing Amy to stir.

"We simply won't know the prognosis for a while. The doctor explained that they have to look at the X-rays to find the extent of the damage. If it hit the bone, surgery might be required. He says there was little loss of blood, which is a very good sign. They've hooked him up with IV antibiotics and fluids. Whatever is decided, he'll need wound treatment and dressings. The ironic part is that he was wearing his bulletproof vest, but it doesn't cover the arms."

Natalie shuddered. "Mrs. Saunders?"

"Call me June."

"June, then. If it hampers his ability to use his arm, will that mean he can't be a Ranger anymore? Because I know that would just about kill him."

"That's my worry, too. We'll simply have to wait and see. On the bright side, you won't have to worry about your safety anymore. Kit took down the man who killed your husband."

Talk about the bitter with the sweet—

"He also killed one of the man's accomplices and wounded another, who has been arrested. Ranger Vance killed the fourth man, the one who was hiding in the getaway car and injured Kit."

It took a minute for Natalie to take it all in. She stared at Kit's mother. "You've been through this before."

"Yes. But this time we can be thankful Kit's life has been spared."

"I—I'm so thankful, I don't know how to react. How terrifying for you to have to hear news like this about your son." Natalie put her arms around the older woman, and the two of them simply held on to each other for a little while before June pulled back, wiping her eyes.

"I've been told your living room window was shattered during the gunfire. It might be best for you to stay here until the Rangers have finished their job and the people from Forensics are through. Then they'll have the mess cleaned up and new glass installed. I imagine that by tomorrow you'll be able to go home."

Natalie felt numb. Home without Kit was unthinkable. "How soon can he have visitors?"

"The surgeon told me not until tomorrow and maybe not even then depending on his condition. He's been through a lot of trauma physically and psychologically."

"But he's tough."

June nodded. "He's just like his father."

"Has your other son been told?"

"Yes. I called Brandon the second I had word from his captain. He'll arrive at the hospital before long to talk to the doctor."

"Why don't you stay here until you hear from him? I was just about to make coffee. Have you had any breakfast?"

"Not yet."

"Then let me get us some. I'm so thankful he's alive, I need to work off my excess energy and stay busy. I'm glad you're here with me. Amy and I would love the company. It's been very quiet with just the two of us."

"It must have been intolerable to be cooped up in your house."

"Not really." *Not at all. I've had Kit all to myself. Now there's no excuse for us to be together under the same roof.* "What I've missed is taking this little girl out to the park."

Amy awakened and stood in the playpen. "Mama." She held out her arms. "Kit!"

"Oh—" June laughed. "She knows his name. She's adorable."

"He's been playing with her." She walked over to the playpen. "Amy, this is June. Can you say June?"

She pointed her finger at Kit's mother. "June."

"Yes, sweetheart. June!" Natalie looked at Kit's mother. "Your son has won her heart. I'll just change her diaper and get her dressed. Then she can eat breakfast with us."

She picked Amy up and carried her into the bathroom. When she returned to the living room she saw that June had gone into the kitchen. She'd made the coffee for them and was toasting Eggo waffles.

"Waffles sound good." Natalie put the baby in the high chair.

"Kit has always loved them."

She got out the syrup and the butter. While June brought the plates of waffles to the table, Natalie found a jar of applesauce she'd brought with her. She broke a waffle into pieces for Amy and June poured the coffee.

They began eating their breakfast, but after a few mouthfuls of fruit, Amy wanted to get down. "My daughter is restless. Excuse me for a minute. I'll put on her sandals and take her outside for a little walk. In the rush to get here yesterday, I forgot to pack the stroller."

"I'll walk outside with you. Right now I'm afraid I can't sit still."

"Neither can I." Their eyes met in silent understanding.

Natalie was hurting for Kit, but she experienced a feeling of liberation to walk outside and know there was no danger lurking. The surveillance van had gone. Amy stopped and started many times, exploring this new world. It caused both women to laugh. Several times she stumbled. Natalie let her pick herself up.

Already too hot to stay out for long, they headed back to the condo. Their return coincided with June's cell phone ringing. She pulled it out of her pocket. "It's Brandon."

"Go ahead and talk while we get ourselves some water." Amy followed Natalie into the kitchen, where Natalie got down a glass and filled it for her. The little girl drank from it very well. Before long she wouldn't need her sippy cup.

June joined them. "I'm going to drive over to the hospital to talk to Brandon, but I'll be back."

"You go and be with your sons. You all need each other."

"Thank you for being so understanding. You're a sweet person, Natalie. I promise I won't be long and I'll bring any news." She gave Natalie another hug and leaned over and kissed Amy's cheek.

"Bye-bye, Amy."

"'Bye, June."

Incredible.

Kit's mother laughed. So did Natalie, who felt as

though ten years had just been added to her daughter's life. They walked June to the door and watched as she drove off. Natalie would give anything to go to the hospital with her, but that wasn't her place. Not until Kit either phoned or got word to her that he wanted her to come.

She closed the door. Only now was it starting to sink in that everything was over and the murder case involving her mentally ill husband had been solved. Life could get back on track. Everything was going to change. No more Kit in the house. She was free to go to work again.

But Natalie realized she didn't want things to change. She wanted to go on living in a world where Kit stayed with her and Amy forever. Her thoughts flew to him. This shooting could have had a life-changing effect on him.

What if the damage to his arm was bad enough that he couldn't be a fully active Texas Ranger anymore? He had to have a full recovery. *He had to.*

Chapter Ten

The doctor walked into Kit's hospital room and approached the side of his bed. "How are you feeling?"

Kit had awakened again and was surprised to discover it was four in the afternoon. "No pain."

"That's good. I'm here to tell you that the bullet perforated your upper arm in the best place it could have. It missed the bone and artery, so there's no need for surgery. We'll be able to treat this as a flesh wound."

"That's the news I've been waiting for. I've got to get back to work." *I've got to get back to Natalie.*

"Not so fast, Ranger Saunders. I won't be releasing you from the hospital until the day after tomorrow. You need bed rest while we tend to your wound and pump you full of more antibiotics. Infection is your biggest enemy. We don't want to give it a chance."

"I can do that at home."

"No you can't. We're keeping you on the IV and the dressings and wound care need to be handled here. I want your blood pressure to go down."

Kit could see this doctor meant business. "Can I have visitors now?"

"Only your immediate family. The whole department of the Texas Rangers has kept our phone ringing off the hook, but none of them except your closest friends are allowed to visit before tomorrow. After I've done my rounds and can see that you're improving, I'll lift the ban. Have I made myself clear?"

He sounded like TJ. "Understood."

"Before you're released, a therapist will be in to discuss your recovery and rehabilitation."

"How long will I have to do therapy?"

"That depends. Several months. I'd say no active field work for at least four, and only on my say-so."

Four? "Be honest with me. When all is said and done, do you think I'll be able to pass the Ranger physical?"

The doctor's brows lifted. "I honestly don't know."

"What's your best guess?"

"We can hope for maybe ninety-five percent."

Kit frowned. "That won't be good enough."

"You just got shot, Ranger Saunders. These things take time."

"Don't I know it," he grumbled. "Can I have my cell phone back?"

"Not before tomorrow. We've turned the landline off in this room, too. After what you've been through, it's vital you get your rest. Take some naps. Watch some TV."

"That's like watching paint dry."

"Exactly. Best therapy in the world." He started for the door.

"Doc?"

The man turned. "What is it?"

Kit knew he'd been rude. "Thank you."

"Just doing my job."

Kit had used that phrase on Natalie several times. He'd never been on the receiving end of it. "Thanks, anyway."

The doctor smiled. "You're welcome."

Left alone for the moment, the only thing that helped Kit handle this enforced bed rest was knowing Morales and his gang were dead or in jail. He was longing to debrief with Cy and Vic, but that would have to wait until tomorrow.

"Kit?" June peeked her head around the door. "Do you mind if we come in?"

"I've been waiting for you."

She came into the room, followed by Brandon. They both walked over to the side of the bed that was free of IV drips and monitors. Kit's brother grinned. "You're looking good for somebody who took down Austin's finest gang of felons. They all had rap sheets a mile long. The news said they came at you with guns blazing, including an AR-15. You've been labeled the new Elliott Ness. Dad's probably upstairs grinning from ear to ear."

"You think?"

His mother leaned over and kissed his cheek. "Thank God you're alive."

"I've been thanking Him."

Brandon said, "I've been thanking Him this didn't happen before my event in San Antonio. You're the best damn hazer I ever worked with."

"That's a compliment I'll remember, but I'm not dead yet. Mom, would you do me a favor and go over to my condo? Natalie's staying there. She needs to know I'm all right and that the worry is over."

"Your captain called me early this morning and I went right over to tell her what I knew. We had breakfast and took a walk with Amy. Natalie taught her my name. You've never seen anything so cute in your life."

Kit could imagine it and felt his eyelids sting with emotion. He had to clear his throat. "How is Natalie?"

"Handling it all like a trooper. She reminded me how strong you are. I needed that. I love both you boys."

Brandon eyed Kit and they exchanged a silent message. They knew this incident had brought their father's death back to their mother. "We love you, too, Mom. Come on. I'll take you out for a steak dinner, then we'll come back to say good-night."

"I'll see you later," Kit murmured, pleased that his mother had spoken to Natalie, but surprised the talking had made him so tired.

NATALIE WAS FEEDING Amy dinner when her cell rang. She clicked on. Maybe it was June. She'd said she'd be coming back. "Hello?"

"Mrs. Harris? This is Cy Vance. I've been at the hospital talking to Mrs. Saunders. She said the doctor won't let anyone talk to Kit on the phone or visit him until tomorrow. When she said she was going back to his condo to give you the latest news, I told her I would do it."

What?

"Your living room has a new window and all the mess has been cleaned up. If you'd like, I'll come by for you in the van and we'll move you back to your house. You and Amy will be able to sleep in your own beds tonight."

She groaned inwardly. The news that she could go home should have brought her relief. But she'd wanted to go to the hospital to tell Kit she'd stay at his place so she could help him when he came home.

"That's very kind of you. Are you coming now?"

"Yes."

"Then I'll gather up our things and be ready for you."

By eight-thirty, Cy had carried the last of the bags into her house. Everything looked as before, as though nothing had ever happened here. She thanked the Ranger profusely for helping her.

"It's the least I can do. Kit's going to be fine—he wouldn't want you to worry. If you need anything, call me."

"Of course. You've been wonderful." She watched him drive away before she closed the front door.

Amy had been playing right by her leg. She picked her up and took her to the nursery. Before long her sweet girl cuddled up in her crib with her cow and fell asleep after only two songs.

Finally alone to think, she phoned Jillian. They had a long talk. Jillian offered to look after Amy so Natalie could visit Kit in the hospital. What a great friend she'd been! She thanked her and rang off. There was one more call to make. Colette needed to know that Kit had solved the case and that a large part of it had been due to her.

Natalie put off calling her boss at the pharmacy. She wanted to see Kit before she committed to going back to work. Kit might need help for a while and she wanted to be the one to provide it. That was, if Kit wanted her to. She'd felt so confident about his feelings when they'd kissed goodbye, she had no idea what sorts of things had been on his mind since he'd been shot. If anything had changed, she wouldn't be able to bear it.

Being in her own bed felt good, but she would rather be at Kit's condo. She loved him so desperately. To think she could have lost him—emotion got the better of her and she started sobbing. And once they'd started, the tears continued to come, drenching her pillow.

THE NEXT DAY Natalie called the hospital, wanting to know when Kit was allowed to have visitors.

She was pleased to learn that she could go in between four and five, and she arranged with Jillian to drop Amy off at three-thirty so she could be at the hospital in good time.

She went through her normal routine with Amy, turning on the TV to have some background noise. There was a soap opera on one of the channels dealing with a case of stolen diamonds that had been hidden on the inside of the fireplace. She didn't think much about it until later when she stood in the shower washing her hair.

What a crazy place to hide something. Natalie was

positive the police hadn't looked inside her fireplace. Who would? But she couldn't let the idea go. After she'd toweled off and dried her hair, she slipped on an old T-shirt and went into the living room. She glanced out the window, feeling a little silly, and removed the fireplace screen, reaching inside the way she'd seen the woman on the show do it.

To her shock she felt a packet pasted against the bricks. She got her fingers around it and pulled hard. Out came two large and very dirty envelopes. Were there more? She reached in again on the other side and pulled out two more. Maybe there were others but she couldn't reach up that far. Good grief.

She took them into the kitchen and opened them on the table. Each packet contained a thick stack of hundred dollar bills, more cash than Natalie had ever seen in her life. Her eyes widened in disbelief. *The $400,000!* They never used the fireplace. Ever. Rod must have stashed the envelopes there, knowing they'd be safe.

Wait till she showed all this to Kit.

Excited about the find, she dug out a small, old suitcase. Kit would want Forensics to match serial numbers and dust the envelopes for prints, so she put all four packets inside and snapped it shut.

She washed her hands and arms up to the elbows then finished dressing. She chose to wear a filmy white blouse and khaki-colored wraparound skirt Kit had never seen. Before she left for the hospital, she walked Amy over to Jillian's. At first Amy acted shy, but then she saw her little friend and wiggled to get out of Natalie's arms.

Natalie hugged her friend and slipped out the front door while her daughter was occupied. She went back to the house and carried the suitcase out to her car. The hospital wasn't far away, but it took time to park.

She rode the east elevator to the fourth floor nursing station. One of the nurses told her that Kit already had visitors, but that Natalie could go in as soon as they left. The doctor didn't want him overly excited.

She had to wait fifteen minutes before being told it was her turn. Timed visits meant the doctor was still worried about him. Natalie's heart pounded as she entered his room, hoping his eyes would reflect his true feelings.

His head was raised, but his eyes were closed when she came in. He must be exhausted. She took in the IV tube and the bandage on his right arm. She walked quietly to his bedside and set down the suitcase.

She loved just looking at him. He was beautiful in a rugged, manly way. He opened his eyes, catching her in the act of feasting her eyes on him, but his gaze reflected concern. Why?

Natalie said the first thing that came into her mind. "You got 'em, cowboy."

He sighed deeply. "Not without help. Cy saved my hide when he told me to duck. If I hadn't…"

"Let's concentrate on the fact that you put away four felons. In honor of that spectacular feat, I have a surprise for you."

"Tell me it's your mint brownies."

"You can't eat those yet, but I've brought something I can guarantee will make you really happy."

"Is it edible?"

"I don't think you'd want to eat it, no. I'll give you a clue. I discovered it while I was watching a soap opera this afternoon. Maybe you saw it, too."

"I slept through reruns of *Bonanza*."

"Well, luckily I didn't sleep through *my* show." She brought the tray table forward, taking care not to disturb the IV. "Are you ready?"

Natalie put the small suitcase on top of the table and opened it.

Kit's eyes flickered then blazed. That's the look she'd wanted to see.

"Four-hundred thousand! It's all there. It was dirty business, but I counted it."

He stared at her. "Where in the hell did you find it?"

"Well, on this program today the culprit hid some diamonds in a packet inside the fireplace. I thought it was hilarious, but then again it was the only place in my house I could think of that hadn't been searched. Just for fun I stuck my hand up the chimney and *voila*!

"Those four dirty envelopes had been fastened to the inside with tape. You can tell your captain you've found the stolen money, at least what's left of those millions. It'll make you a bigger hero than you already are. I'll never say a word. But that's enough excitement for now."

She closed the lid and put the case back on the floor, then moved the table away.

When she returned to his side, he reached for her

hand and clasped it hard. "When the captain finds out, he'll make you a Ranger."

"Oh, no, there's only one Texas Ranger in our family." She'd been so happy, she'd gotten carried away, said something she hadn't meant to say out loud.

"I heard that," he said softly. "You *can't* take it back."

Natalie's mouth went so dry she could hardly swallow. "I don't want to. I love you, Kit. I've been in love with you from the start. I would never have agreed for Father Segal to live with me if I hadn't sensed I'd met the love of my life.

"I was afraid you'd think badly of me for having been married to a killer. The thought is so distasteful to me, I can't imagine what kind of thoughts you must have had at the beginning."

"If you'll lean over and kiss me, I'll give you an idea of what my thoughts were when you invited me into your house for the first time."

Natalie was already there. "I adore you," she whispered. "I'm glad you're a Ranger. I'll never complain about you going out on a case, as long as you always come home to me."

"I promise I will always come home to you, Natalie. Marry me. Right away—I mean it. We'll work out all the details later, but I want everyone to know you're going to be my wife."

"People are going to think we're rushing things."

"I don't care what anyone else thinks. I've been waiting for you for years."

"Oh, Kit—" Tears rolled down her cheeks. "I hated

to leave your condo yesterday. I wanted to be there when you got out of the hospital, but Cy showed up to help me move my things back home."

"I asked him to do it."

She kissed his mouth again. "Why?"

"Because I want to spend my convalescence at your house where Amy is happy. We'll have my couch brought over and I'll sleep on it. That town house is no good to us, anyway. I've been thinking about buying some property with acreage for horses. We're going to need a much bigger house."

Natalie smiled. "How big?"

"With enough bedrooms for more children. I'd like to hire an architect to design a Western-style home with lots of windows and timber."

"That'll be a project to keep you busy until you're back on the force."

"I'm afraid that's still iffy."

"No, it's not. You'll be back in no time."

He caressed the side of her face. "What did I ever do to deserve you?"

"You've got that the other way around." They couldn't stop kissing each other.

"My mother's already crazy about Amy."

"It was so funny yesterday. Oh, Kit—we can't wait for you to come home."

"One more night, then we'll never be apart again."

That sounded like heaven.

Epilogue

Tonight was their three-month wedding anniversary.

Natalie had prepared a special picnic and had driven to the new house they were building in Barton Creek. Kit had gone in for his physical and planned to meet her there afterward. She was nervous waiting to hear the verdict.

This morning his mother had come to Natalie's house and told her she wanted to look after Amy overnight. Whatever news Kit received, June knew how important this night was to the two of them. She wanted to give them time alone. Natalie had learned to love his mother and Amy was crazy about her nana. There'd be no more calling her "June."

The framework of the two-story ranch house had been erected. The drywall would go in next. Natalie walked inside. The front door hadn't been hung yet. She went up the staircase to the master bedroom where the adjoining veranda looked out over their ten-acre estate. Kit would only be seven miles from work, yet it felt as if they were far away from civilization.

As soon as the barn was built, Kit would bring

his horse from Marble Falls and buy one for Natalie.
Vic had purchased a miniature horse for his son. Kit
couldn't wait to get one for Amy, but she needed to be a
little older first. He planned to take the daughter he was
adopting on rides around the property. With the sixty-
thousand-dollar trust fund she'd inherited, Amy could
one day study to be anything she wanted—maybe an
architect, like her great-grandfather. But secretly Natalie knew that Kit wanted to turn his little cherub into
a cowgirl. Natalie loved the idea.

In a few minutes she glimpsed Kit's car through the
trees, coming up the winding drive. Her heart picked
up speed. *Please let him bring the news he wanted.*
They'd both stayed busy getting this house designed
and built, but she knew he couldn't wait to be back
with the Sons of the Forty.

His Ranger friends dropped in whenever they could,
but when they were on a new case, Kit might not see
them for weeks at a time. He'd been going to his therapy sessions faithfully and doing everything possible
to hasten the healing process.

But sometimes he would get discouraged. He didn't
know if he could handle a desk job for the Rangers.
That rush he got when he went out on a case would always be missing. About a month ago he was having a
bad night and she'd asked him if he'd be interested in
forming a private investigator agency. He would own it
and run in a way only he knew how to make it successful. To her surprise, he didn't dismiss her suggestion.
Just to know he was considering the idea gave her hope.

She watched him pull up and get out of the car. His

body language gave her the first indication that he wasn't happy. Her stomach clenched. She would have to be strong for him.

"Natalie?" Excitement was missing from his voice.

"I'm up in our bedroom, babe." She'd brought blankets and their sleeping bags so they could spend the night. With her heart pounding, she waited in the bedroom for him. He walked in and his gaze darted to the picnic she'd laid out. He took in the sleeping bags.

"Tell me what the doctor said."

His wooden expression said it all. "I'm not there yet."

"You'll get there. When does he want to see you again?"

"In a month."

"That's not a long time. Another month of therapy will make you stronger. By then our house will be finished and you'll be able to get back to work."

He nodded before his hands went to his hips. He was so gorgeous and she loved him desperately, but she couldn't help him.

"Come on. The sun is setting. Let's eat while we can still see our food." She'd made his favorite fried chicken and brownies, but there was no tempting him.

"I'm afraid I'm not hungry."

"That's okay. Shall we go to a roadhouse and do some line dancing? Your mom is keeping Amy overnight. We're free to do whatever we want."

"Natalie?" His eyes were like lasers. "I'm afraid you've married a failure."

She smiled and crossed the distance to press a kiss

to his mouth. "What's that awful cliché? It's always darkest before the dawn. Your day is coming."

He suddenly clasped her to him and buried his face in her hair. "What am I doing? You're so wonderful. How can you stand me while I'm feeling so sorry for myself? Forgive me, sweetheart."

"There's nothing to forgive."

"I love you." His fierce declaration was followed by a kiss to die for. They sank onto the double sleeping bag and clothes flew in all directions. Natalie lost awareness of time and place as Kit made sweet, savage love to her. Then it was her turn to worship him. The joy they brought each other went until late into the night.

She rested against his chest. "Are you hungry?"

"I think I am."

"Stay there." She reached for the cooler and pulled it close. "What would you like? How about a drumstick?" His appetite had come alive. He quickly ate everything she put in front of him, including all the brownies. But she didn't want any food.

"My, my. You really *were* hungry. I think you're ready to handle my news."

She could almost hear his brain turning her comment over. "You've decided to go back to work part-time?"

"No. I don't think I'll be going anywhere for a long time."

"I hate to admit it, but that makes me happy. What caused you to make that decision?"

"The truth is, Kit, this night is special in more ways than one. We're going to have a baby."

He jackknifed into a sitting position. "Natalie—"

"I haven't been to the doctor yet, but I know the signs. It's just like it was with Amy. Please tell me you're happy about it."

"*Happy?* Sweetheart, I'm overjoyed!"

She lay still as he ran his hand over her stomach. "Our little baby is inside there. I've dreamed about having another cherub."

"You're not just saying that?"

"How can you even ask that question?"

"Because I know you're upset that your career is still up in the air."

He kissed her neck. "Hearing that we're going to have a baby puts everything else into perspective. Another month and I'll know if I have to think about other work. Until then I'm going to do what I can to get better. Amy's going to have a little brother or sister. I can't wait!"

"I can't wait until the morning sickness passes. You're so lucky you're a man."

Deep laughter rumbled out of him; the kind she hadn't heard for a long time. She was thrilled.

"Ranger Saunders? Welcome back to active duty." The boss had assembled some of the Rangers in the conference room at the last minute.

"You've only been gone four months, but you've been busy in that time—you've gotten married, built a new house. Is there any other news we need to know about?"

Kit sat back with a smile. "We're expecting a baby in about six months."

The guys hooted and cheered. TJ smiled. "Kit and Cy both went undercover on different assignments and look what happened—they married the women they were protecting. Here's an APB for the rest of you single Rangers—watch out if you decide to go undercover to protect a woman in jeopardy. Okay. Get out of here."

Kit smiled at Cy as they left the room. Before they went their separate ways Cy said, "I'm glad you crossed the line, bud. Always go with your instincts."

"Back at you."

Only seven miles and he'd be home. Natalie didn't yet know he'd gotten the call from TJ saying he'd passed the physical. Kit couldn't wait to tell his wonderful wife, who'd never given up or let him lose hope. She was a gift.

He turned onto the road leading to the house. When he passed through the trees he saw Natalie up on the veranda. It was her favorite place to be. They kept a high chair up there and he could see Amy enjoying her dinner.

"Natalie!" He called to her and raced inside the house. Taking the stairs two at a time he ran through the hall and into their bedroom. She was there to meet him.

"You're back on the force!"

"How did you know? It was supposed to be a surprise."

She kissed him passionately. "A wife just senses these things."

"Dada!" Amy called out.

He turned to kiss his daughter. Life didn't get better than this.

* * * * *

Watch for the final story in Rebecca Winters's
LONE STAR LAWMEN *miniseries,*
HER TEXAS RANGER HERO,
coming September 2016!

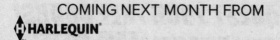

REQUEST YOUR FREE BOOKS!
2 FREE NOVELS PLUS 2 FREE GIFTS!

✦ HARLEQUIN®

American Romance®

LOVE, HOME & HAPPINESS

YES! Please send me 2 FREE Harlequin® American Romance® novels and my 2 FREE gifts (gifts are worth about $10). After receiving them, if I don't wish to receive any more books, I can return the shipping statement marked "cancel." If I don't cancel, I will receive 4 brand-new novels every month and be billed just $4.74 per book in the U.S. or $5.49 per book in Canada. That's a savings of at least 12% off the cover price! It's quite a bargain! Shipping and handling is just 50¢ per book in the U.S. and 75¢ per book in Canada.* I understand that accepting the 2 free books and gifts places me under no obligation to buy anything. I can always return a shipment and cancel at any time. Even if I never buy another book, the two free books and gifts are mine to keep forever.

154/354 HDN GHZZ

Name _____ (PLEASE PRINT) _____

Address _____ Apt. # _____

City _____ State/Prov. _____ Zip/Postal Code _____

Signature (if under 18, a parent or guardian must sign) _____

Mail to the **Reader Service:**
IN U.S.A.: P.O. Box 1867, Buffalo, NY 14240-1867
IN CANADA: P.O. Box 609, Fort Erie, Ontario L2A 5X3

Want to try two free books from another line?
Call 1-800-873-8635 or visit www.ReaderService.com.

* Terms and prices subject to change without notice. Prices do not include applicable taxes. Sales tax applicable in N.Y. Canadian residents will be charged applicable taxes. Offer not valid in Quebec. This offer is limited to one order per household. Not valid for current subscribers to Harlequin American Romance books. All orders subject to credit approval. Credit or debit balances in a customer's account(s) may be offset by any other outstanding balance owed by or to the customer. Please allow 4 to 6 weeks for delivery. Offer available while quantities last.

Your Privacy—The Reader Service is committed to protecting your privacy. Our Privacy Policy is available online at www.ReaderService.com or upon request from the Reader Service.

We make a portion of our mailing list available to reputable third parties that offer products we believe may interest you. If you prefer that we not exchange your name with third parties, or if you wish to clarify or modify your communication preferences, please visit us at www.ReaderService.com/consumerschoice or write to us at Reader Service Preference Service, P.O. Box 9062, Buffalo, NY 14240-9062. Include your complete name and address.

When a one-night stand with Violet Hathaway results in
an unexpected pregnancy, Cole Dempsey must put his
rodeo past behind him and embrace his new life as a
cattle rancher...or lose the woman he loves.

Read on for a sneak peak at
HAVING THE RANCHER'S BABY,
by Cathy McDavid from her
***MUSTANG VALLEY** miniseries!*

"What are you doing here on your day off?" he asked.
"It's Sunday. The day of rest."

"Yeah, well, no rest for the wicked."

He let his voice drop and his eyes rove her face. "You're
not wicked, Vi." Though she could be flirtatious and fun
when she let loose.

For the briefest of seconds, she went still. Then—
strange for her, as Violet usually oozed confidence—she
turned away. "I asked you not to call me that."

"I like Vi. It suits you."

And it was personal. Something just the two of them
shared. Calling her Vi was his way of reminding her
about the night they'd spent together, which he supposed
explained her displeasure. She didn't like being reminded.

She'd made the mistake of telling him that Vi was a
childhood nickname, one she'd insisted on leaving behind
upon entering her teens. They'd been alone, lying in bed
and revealing their innermost feelings. Unfortunately, the
shared intimacy hadn't lasted, disappearing with the first
rays of morning sunlight.

"I was wondering. If you weren't busy later…" She let the sentence drop.

"I'm not busy." Cole leaned closer, suddenly eager. "What do you have in mind?"

Could she have had a change of heart? They weren't supposed to see each other again socially or bring up their one moment of weakness. According to Vi, it had been a mistake. A rash action resulting from two shots of tequila each, a crowded dance floor and both of them weary of constantly fighting their personal demons.

Cole didn't necessarily agree. Sure, the road was not without obstacles. As one of the ranch owners, he was her boss. On the other hand, *she* oversaw *his* work while he learned the ropes. Confusing and awkward and a reason not to date.

But incredible lovemaking and easy conversation didn't happen between just any two people. He and Vi had something special, and he'd have liked to see where it went, obstacles be damned.

Strange, he hadn't given her a second thought before their "mistake." One moment on a dance floor and, boom, everything had changed. A shame she didn't feel the same.

Unless she did and was better at hiding it? The possibility warranted consideration.

"We need to, um, talk." She closed her eyes and pressed a hand to her belly.

Don't miss
HAVING THE RANCHER'S BABY
by Cathy McDavid, available June 2016
wherever Harlequin® American Romance®
books and ebooks are sold.

www.Harlequin.com

Same great stories, new name!

In July 2016,
the HARLEQUIN®
AMERICAN ROMANCE® series
will become
the HARLEQUIN®
WESTERN ROMANCE series.

Connect with us to find your next great read, special offers and more.

 /HarlequinBooks

@HarlequinBooks

www.HarlequinBlog.com

www.Harlequin.com/Newsletters

HARLEQUIN®

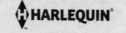 A *Romance* FOR EVERY MOOD™

www.Harlequin.com

New York Times bestselling author

JODI THOMAS

presents another breathtaking
***Ransom Canyon* romance.**

**In this remote west Texas town, where family bonds
are made and broken and young love sparks as
old flames grow dim, Ransom Canyon is ready to
welcome—and shelter—those who need it.**

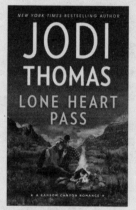

With a career and a relationship in ruins, Jubilee Hamilton is left reeling from a fast fall to the bottom. The run-down Texas farm she's inherited is a far cry from the second chance she hoped for, but it and the abrasive foreman she's forced to hire are all she's got.

Every time Charley Collins has let a woman get close, he's been burned. So Lone Heart ranch and the contrary woman who owns it are merely a means to an end, until Jubilee tempts him to take another risk—to stop resisting the attraction drawing them together despite all his hard-learned logic.

Desperation is all young Thatcher Jones knows. And when he finds himself mixed up in a murder investigation, his only protection is the shelter of a man and woman who—just like him—need someone to trust.

Pick up your copy today!

Be sure to connect with us at:

Harlequin.com/Newsletters
Facebook.com/HarlequinBooks
Twitter.com/HQNBooks

Turn your love of reading into rewards you'll love with

Harlequin My Rewards

**Join for FREE today at
www.HarlequinMyRewards.com**

Earn **FREE BOOKS** of your choice.

Experience **EXCLUSIVE OFFERS** and contests.

Enjoy **BOOK RECOMMENDATIONS**
selected just for you.

PLUS! Sign up now
and get **500** points
right away!

Earn **FREE** REWARDS
HarlequinMyRewards.com
Join Today!